S.R

MARRYING HIS MAJESTY

She'll be his bride—by royal decree!

The crowns of the Diamond Isles are about to return to their rightful heirs: three gorgeous Mediterranean princes. But their road to royal matrimony is lined with secrets, lies and forbidden love…

CLAIMED: SECRET ROYAL SON

A year ago Lily became accidentally pregnant with Prince Alexandros's baby, Now Alex wants to claim his secret royal son, and a convenient wife!

BETROTHED: TO THE PEOPLE'S PRINCE

Nikos is the people's prince, but the crown of Argyros belongs to reluctant Princess, Athena— the woman he was forbidden to marry. Can Nikos finally persuade her to come home?

CROWNED: THE PALACE NANNY

For Elsa, nanny to the nine-year-old heiress to the throne of Khryseis, Zoe, there's more in store than going to the ball. This Cinderella is about to win the heart of the new Prince Regent.

Join Marion Lennox on the Diamond Isles, for three resplendent royal romances!

Dear Reader

Do you have a place of refuge, a haven of exotic beauty for when you most need it? A place where men are men, and know how to romance a woman with true royal fantasy?

I do.

When there's sleet and frost and biting winds, I curl up by the fire (where my dog, Mitzi, and cat, Tigger, soak up most of the heat) and dream of the fabulous Diamond Isles. When it's scorching hot and dusty, and the rattle of everyday life gets to me, I pour myself a long, cool drink, curl up under a shady tree and float away to my glittering royal isles.

The Diamond Isles are three magical islands in the Mediterranean: the Sapphire Isle, the Isle of Silver and the Isle of Gold. Beautiful private beaches with golden sand, glittering turquoise water, gentle breezes, palaces soaring from craggy cliffs, tanned waiters carrying drinks with little umbrellas…a retreat indeed.

On the Diamond Isles we'll find three gorgeous royals, my Island Guardians: the autocratic Prince Alexandros of the Sapphire Isle, rugged Prince Nikos of the Isle of Silver and sophisticated Prince Stefanos of the Isle of Gold. Three men, three heroes, who—each in his own way—will fight to keep his island safe, and who with equal passion will woo his chosen woman and hold her close.

So come away with me to my Diamond Isles, deliciously wrapped in a royal fantasy. I'm so happy you can join me. We won't even need to compete with Mitzi and Tigger for heat—there's more than enough to share...

Marion

CLAIMED:
SECRET ROYAL SON

BY
MARION LENNOX

™ MILLS & BOON®
Pure reading pleasure™

First published in Great Britain 2009
Harlequin Mills & Boon Limited,
Eton House, 18-24 Paradise Road, Richmond, Surrey TW9 1SR

© Marion Lennox 2009

ISBN: 978 0 263 20811 5

Set in Times Roman 10¼ on 12 pt
07-0709-49845

Printed and bound in Great Britain
by CPI Antony Rowe, Chippenham, Wiltshire

Marion Lennox is a country girl, born on an Australian dairy farm. She moved on—mostly because the cows just weren't interested in her stories! Married to a 'very special doctor', Marion writes Mills & Boon® Romance as well as Medical™ Romance. (She used a different name for each category for a while—if you're looking for her past Mills & Boon® Romances, search for author Trisha David as well.) She's now had over 75 romance novels accepted for publication.

In her non-writing life Marion cares for kids, cats, dogs, chooks and goldfish. She travels, and she fights her rampant garden (she's losing) and her house dust (she's lost). Having spun in circles for the first part of her life, she's now stepped back from her 'other' career, which was teaching statistics at her local university. Finally she's reprioritised her life, figured out what's important, and discovered the joys of deep baths, romance and chocolate. Preferably all at the same time!

To Sheila, who makes my books better. With gratitude.

CHAPTER ONE

'WAKE up, Lily.'

There were two doctors and four nurses gathered by the bed. This had been groundbreaking surgery. Heroic stuff. If Lily hadn't been close to death already, they'd never have tried it.

After the operation she'd been kept in an induced coma to give her damaged brain time to recover. They'd saved her life, but would she wake up…whole?

The junior nurse—the gofer in this small, exclusive French hospital—had nothing to do right now and she was free to think about the patient. She'd seen this girl come in a month ago, deeply unconscious, drifting towards death. Rumour said she was related to royalty, but no one came near her.

A nurse was supposed to be objective. She wasn't supposed to care.

There wasn't one person around this bed who didn't care.

'Wake up, Lily,' the surgeon said again, pressing his patient's hand. 'The operation's over. It was a huge success. You're going to be okay.'

And finally Lily's eyelids fluttered open.

She had dark eyes. Brown. Too big for her face.

Confused.

'Hey,' the surgeon said and smiled. 'Hello, Lily.'

'H… Hello.' It was a faint whisper, as if she'd forgotten how to speak.

'How many fingers am I holding up?'

'Three,' she said, not interested.

'That's great,' the surgeon said, jubilant. 'You've been ill—really ill—but we've operated and the tumour's been completely removed. You're going to live.'

Lily's gaze was moving around the room, taking in each person. The medical uniforms. The eager, interested faces.

And then, as if she'd remembered something really important, her eyes widened. Fearful.

'Are you in pain?' the surgeon asked. 'What hurts, Lily?'

'Nothing hurts. But…' Her hand shifted, slow from disuse, and her fingers spread over her abdomen.

'Where's my baby?'

CHAPTER TWO

'I, ALEXANDROS KOSTANTINOS MYKONIS, do swear to govern the peoples of the United Isles of Diamas—the Diamond Isles—on behalf of my infant cousin Michales, until such time as he reaches twenty-five years of age.'

Alex's black uniform was slashed with inserts of crimson and richly adorned with braid, tassels and medals. A lethal-looking sword hung by his side, its golden grip emblazoned with the royal coat of arms. His snug black-as-night trousers looked sexy-as-hell, and his leather boots were so shiny a girl could see her face in them.

If she got close enough. As once she'd been close.

Lily could barely see Alex's face from where she watched in the further-most corner of the cathedral, but she knew every inch of his hawk-like features. His brown-black eyes were some-times creased with laughter, yet sometimes seemed so severe she'd think he carried the weight of the world on his shoulders.

It had been wonderful to make him smile. He'd made her smile, too.

He'd melted her heart—or she thought he had. Love was all about trust, and trust was stupid. She'd learned that now, but what a way to learn.

She watched on, numbed by the day's events. Shocked. Be-wildered. Trying desperately to focus on what was happening.

The ring, the glove, the royal stole, the rod with the dove, were bestowed on Alex with gravity, and with gravity he accepted them. This coronation ceremony was as it had been for generations. Alex looked calm, assured and regal.

The last time she'd seen him he'd been in her bed, leaning over her in the aftermath of loving. His eyes had been wicked with laughter. His jeans and shirt had been crumpled on the floor.

Alexandros Mykonis. Successful landscape architect, internationally acclaimed. Her one-time lover.

The new Prince Regent of the Diamond Isles.

The father of her baby.

'Doesn't he look fabulous?' The woman sitting next to her— a reporter, according to the press pass round her neck—was sighing mistily as Alex knelt to receive the blessing.

'He does,' Lily whispered back.

They watched on. He was well worth watching.

The blessing over, Alex rose and proceeded to sign the royal deeds of office. Trumpeters, organist and choir filled the church with triumphant chorus, but there was room within the music's shadow for talk.

'There's not a single woman here who doesn't think he's hot,' the reporter whispered.

Lily hesitated. She should keep quiet, but she was here with a purpose. If she were to get her baby back she needed all the information she could gather. 'It's a wonder he's not married,' she ventured.

'He's not the marrying kind,' the reporter told her, sighing again with the waste of it. 'Though not for want of interest. There's always been some woman or other. My guess is he's disillusioned. His father, King Giorgos's brother, disobeyed royal orders and married for love, but the marriage caused nothing but grief.'

'Why?' she asked, but before the reporter could answer they were distracted.

The Archbishop, magnificent in his gold and white ecclesiastical gowns, had handed newly signed documents to an elderly priest.

The priest, a bit doddery and clearly nervous, took the documents with fumbling fingers—and dropped them.

'That's Father Antonio,' the reporter whispered as the old priest stared down at the scattered papers in dismay. 'He's been the island's priest for as long as I can remember. The Archbishop didn't want him to be part of this ceremony, but Prince Alexandros insisted.'

The old priest was on his knees, trying to gather the scattered documents, clearly distressed. Instead of helping, the Archbishop looked on with distaste. Following his lead, the other officials did nothing.

It was Alex who came to his rescue. As if this pomp and ceremony was an everyday occurrence, he stooped to help gather the papers, then helped the old man to his feet.

Then, as the old priest's face worked, trying desperately to contain his distress at his clumsiness, Alex set his hands on his shoulders and he kissed him. Once on each cheek, in the age-old way of the men of this island.

It was a gesture of affection and of respect.

It was a gesture to restore dignity.

'Thank you, Father,' Alex said simply, his deep voice resonating throughout the church. 'You've looked after the islanders well during my whole life. You baptised me, you buried my parents, and now you do me honour by being here. You have my gratitude.'

He smiled, and almost every woman in the cathedral sighed and smiled in unison.

'See, that's why the islanders love him,' the reporter whispered, smiling mistily herself. 'That's why the islanders would have loved him to take the throne himself. If only this baby hadn't been born. Who'd have expected the old King to get himself a son at his age? He only did it to block Alex from the succession. His marriage to Mia was a farce.'

But Lily was no longer listening. That smile…that gentleness…

She'd forgotten, she thought, blinking back involuntary tears. She'd forgotten why she'd lost her heart.

She was being dumb. Emotional. She needed to gather information and move on. She needed to stay detached.

Impossible, but she had to try.

'What happened with his parents' marriage?' she managed.

The reporter was gazing adoringly at Alex but she was still willing to talk, and she hadn't lost the thread of their conversation.

'Horrid story,' she said absently. 'Alex was their only child. Because his father was Giorgos's brother and Giorgos was childless, until this baby was born Alex was heir to his uncle's throne. When Alex was five his father drowned, and Giorgos banished his mother from the island. But because Alex was his heir, he kept him. He didn't care for him, though. Alex was brought up in isolation at the castle. When he was fifteen rumour has it that he stood up to his uncle— I have no idea what he threatened him with but it worked. His mother was allowed back. She and Alex went to live in their old home but she died soon after. They say Alex hated his uncle for it—they say he hated everything to do with royalty. But now he's stuck, minding the throne for this baby but with no real power himself.'

Suddenly the reporter's focus was distracted. Some angle of light—something—had redirected her attention to Lily. A glance become a stare. 'Do I know you?' she demanded. 'You look familiar.'

Uh-oh. She shouldn't have talked. Not here, not at such close quarters where she could be studied. 'I don't think so.' She tugged her scarf further down over her tight-cropped curls and pretended to be absorbed in the proceedings again.

'I'm sure I know you.' The girl was still staring.

'You don't,' she said bluntly. 'I only arrived this morning.' To shock, to heartache and to confusion.

'You're a relative? A friend? An official?' The girl was looking at her clothes. They were hardly suitable for such an event. She'd done her best, but her best was shabby. She'd gone for a plain and simple black skirt and jacket, a bit loose now on her too-thin frame. Her only indulgence was her scarf. It was tie-dyed silk, like a Monet landscape, a lovely confection of rose and blue and palest lemon.

She knew she didn't fit in with these glamorous people from all around the world. How anyone could link her with her older sister…

'You look like the Queen,' the girl said, and it took all her control to stop herself flinching.

'I'm sure I don't.'

'You're not related?'

She made herself smile. 'How could you think that?' she managed. 'Queen Mia is so glamorous.'

'But she's abandoned her baby,' the reporter whispered, distracted from Alex's romantic background and filled with indignation for a more recent scandal. 'Can you imagine? The King dies and Mia walks away with one of the world's richest men. Leaving her baby.'

Her baby. *Her* baby!

But still the girl was staring. She had to deflect the attention somehow. 'I'm here in an official capacity,' she told the reporter bluntly, in a voice that said *no more questions*.

She fingered the gilt invitation in her jacket pocket. When she'd arrived—in those first few dreadful minutes when she'd realised what Mia had done—she'd half expected to be turned away. But Mia had invited her and apparently she was still on the official guest list. Alex had probably long forgotten her existence. Her papers were in order. Her invitation was real. There was no problem.

Ha! There were problems everywhere. Where to go from here?

A trumpet was sounding alone now, a glorious blaze of sound that had the congregation on their feet, applauding the new Prince Regent. Prince Alexandros of the Diamond Isles swept down the aisle, looking every inch a monarch, every inch a royal. Looking worlds away from the Alex she'd fallen in love with.

He was smiling, glancing from side to side as he passed, making eye contact with everyone.

He'd be a much better ruler than the old King, Lily thought, feeling dazed. He'd be a man of the people. Others were clapping and so did she.

His gaze swept past her—and stopped. There was a flicker of recognition.

His smile faded.

She closed her eyes.

When she opened them he'd passed, but once again the reporter looked at her, her face alive with curiosity.

'He knew you,' she breathed.

'I've met him…once.'

'Excuse me, but he looked like he hated you,' the girl said.

'Well, that would be a nonsense,' Lily managed. 'He hardly knows me and I hardly know him. Now, if you'll excuse me…'

She turned her back on the girl and joined the slow procession out into the morning sunshine. Only she knew how hard it was to walk. Only she knew her knees had turned to jelly.

She was here for her baby, but all she wanted was to run.

What the hell was she doing here?

Alex shook one hand after another, so many hands his arms

ached. His smile stayed pinned in place by sheer willpower. Would this day never end?

And what was Lily doing here?

He'd met her once, for two days only. For a short, sweet time he'd thought it could be different. It could be...something. But then she'd left without goodbyes, slipping away in the pre-dawn light and catching the ferry to Athens before he'd woken.

It hadn't stopped him looking for her—up and down the Eastern seaboard of the United States, searching for the sister of the Queen, who he'd been told was a boat-builder.

He hardly believed the boat-builder bit. When he'd asked Mia she'd simply shrugged. 'My parents separated. I went with my mother, but Lily chose to stay with my father, so I've barely seen her since childhood. Her whereabouts and what she does is therefore not my concern. I don't see why it should be yours.'

Undeterred, he'd kept searching. He'd finally found her employer—an elderly Greek boat-builder based in Maine, who'd eyed him up and down and decided to be honest.

'Yes, I employ Lily, but she won't thank me for admitting she's the Queen's sister. No one here knows the connection except my family. And, as for telling you where she is... In honesty, my friend, I don't know. She left here a month ago, pleading ill health. She gets headaches—bad ones—and they're getting worse. We told her to take a break, get healthy and come back to us. My wife is worried about her. We're keeping her apartment over our yard because we value her, but for now...she's gone and we don't know where.'

So he'd been left—again—with the searing sense of loss that was grief. He'd lost his father when he was five and the old King had torn him from his mother. When finally he'd been old enough to make choices for himself, he'd been reunited with his mother, only to have her die as well.

He'd been gutted. The old King's cruelty cut deep. He'd sworn at his mother's graveside not to get attached again. He'd sworn to have as little as possible to do with royalty.

But somehow the Queen's sister had slipped under his defences.

While they'd made love…while they'd talked and laughed into the night…while he'd held her close and listened to her heartbeat…while he'd felt the wonder of their bodies merging as if they were one…it had seemed then as if she was falling for him as hard as he was falling for her. But in the end, for Lily, it must have been a mere one-night stand. Like her sister, was she just after scalps?

The memory of his useless vow had slammed back, mocking him.

Then she'd phoned.

He'd been back in Manhattan, getting on with his life. It had been mid-morning. He'd just fielded a stressful call. He'd still been feeling irritated that Lily so obviously hadn't wanted to be found. He'd been caught off guard and he'd made a stupid joke.

Okay, it had been the wrong thing to joke about. It had been crude, but she hadn't given him a chance to apologise. She'd cut the connection. That had been that.

He'd never wanted to fall for her in the first place. Dammit, he did not want to get emotionally involved, especially with someone connected to Mia.

Somehow she'd breached his defences, but that was a mistake. His defences had to get stronger.

So now, for her to turn up here, today…

He was doing all the right things, saying the right things, moving through the crowd with practised ease, but all the time he was looking out for her. A woman dressed in a drab black suit with a crazy scarf…

'Hey, Alex, look at you.' It was Nikos, and Stefanos was right behind him. As a kid, these two had been his best friends. Stefanos was from Khryseis, Nikos was from Argyros.

'When we grow up we'll rule the islands together,' they'd declared. Even as teenagers, they'd dreamed.

Once upon a time the Diamond Isles had been ruled as three principalities; Sappheiros, Khryseis and Argyros—the Isles of Sapphire, Gold and Silver. Then, two hundred years back, the Crown Prince of Sappheiros had invaded his neighbours. He'd taken control and rewritten the constitution. For as long as he had a direct male heir, the islands would be ruled as one kingdom.

For generations, successive kings had bled the islands dry. Finally came Giorgos, a weak excuse for a monarch. He also had no interest in women, and for years it appeared he'd be the last of the direct line. The islanders had held their collective breath.

Alex and Nikos and Stefanos had held their breath.

Alex had stood to inherit the crown of Sappheiros—as Giorgos's nephew and legitimate heir. Stefanos stood one step back from inheriting the Isle of Khryseis, and Nikos might as well be ruler of Argyros. They were strong men with a common purpose. When the old King died, when the islands reverted to being independent nations, they'd rebuild their economies, they'd stop the siphoning of wealth to the royals and they'd form democracies.

But then, stunningly, Giorgos had married Mia, a woman forty years his junior—and Mia had produced a son. The old rule prevailed. As Giorgos's nephew, Alex could rule, but only as Prince Regent until the baby came of age. The baby would be the next King.

So he was stuck, Alex thought, still watching for Lily, still distracted by his friends but never getting away from his overriding disgust at the way things had played out. He'd be playing father to the child of a man he'd loathed. He'd be playing Prince

Regent to a country whose rule he despised, with no authority to change things. And his friends… Behind their smiles there was desperation. They hid it as they'd always hidden it. With humour and false bravado.

'Hey, look at you!' Stefanos exclaimed, clapping his hand on Alex's shoulder. 'One more tassel and you'll be declared a Christmas tree.'

'All you need is some fairy lights,' Nikos agreed, laughing. 'Hey…'

'Mia's sister's here,' he said before they could continue. 'Lily.'

Their banter ceased. They were great friends, Alex thought. If this baby hadn't been born, how much good could they have done?

These two had met Lily. They'd seen how he felt about her. Maybe his feelings were still showing in his face, but he couldn't prevent them.

'Why the hell…?' Nikos demanded, looking round. 'I can't see her.'

'She's playing a drab country mouse—black skirt and jacket, and a scarf over her hair. I guess she thinks it'll stop people recognising her.'

'She has a nerve coming here,' Stefanos said. 'If the people knew… They're aching to lynch Mia.'

'Lily's not Mia.'

'I seem to remember she wound you round her little finger,' Nikos said, still smiling, but his eyes were watchful and tinged with sympathy.

'Yeah, I fell hard,' Alex said, trying to make his voice light. 'I was conned, as Giorgos was conned.'

'Hey, Mia didn't con him. She married him and she bore his child.'

'She married for power and position.'

'And you fell for the sister.'

'It was little more than a one-night stand. Why the hell's she here?'

'Ask her.'

'I guess I must,' he said heavily. 'If Lily thinks she can still play at being part of the royal family…'

'You'll set her right?' Stefanos asked.

'Of course I will,' Alex said heavily. 'And then she'll leave.'

A royal birth, a royal death and a baby abandoned by a royal mother… It had taken Lily most of the day to figure out exactly what had happened.

She'd listened. She'd asked discreet questions of other guests, and she was appalled. She knew enough now to realise the islanders were almost as appalled as she was. There was massive dissent. One more shock might well bring down the monarchy and, for some reason she hadn't figured out, that'd be a disaster.

But it couldn't matter, Lily thought bleakly as the day wore on and she sifted information. She wasn't royal but she wanted the baby. She wanted *her* baby.

Finally she made her way to the nursery. She found it simply by asking for directions from a maid, sounding authoritative, then slipping quietly in without asking.

The nursery was empty, apart from its tiny prince.

Michales was sleeping. He was tucked on his side in his crib, rolled in a soft fuzz of blanket, sucking his thumb in sleep. He had a thatch of thick black curls, amazing for a baby so young. His long lashes fluttered over his tiny cheeks as he slept.

He was…beautiful.

He was hers.

Michales, named after her father, Michael. That was the only promise Mia had kept.

Over the last few weeks she'd wondered how she'd feel when she first saw him, but now, as she gazed at her sleeping son she knew what she felt. Anger? Betrayal? Yes, both of those, but overriding everything…love. He was perfect, she thought in wonder as she gazed down at her sleeping baby.

Her son. Her baby. Michales.

'What the hell are you doing?'

Alex's voice made her jump. Everything about this man made her jump. He was like a panther, moving with stealth wherever he was least expected. She whirled and found him watching from the doorway, his face impassive.

Twelve months ago she'd found him irresistible. Drop dead gorgeous. Passionate. Even tender.

Now he just looked angry. Regally angry. So far from the Alex she remembered that she cringed.

'I came… I came to see my sister,' she managed.

'As you see—Mia's gone. Abandoning her baby. Abandoning everything to join a man so rich he can buy what she thinks she deserves. Are you saying you didn't know?'

'I didn't.' She fingered the invitation in her pocket, fighting for courage. The anger on Alex's face was enough to frighten a braver woman than she was. 'She asked me to come. She sent me an invitation. I arrived this morning to find her…'

'Gone,' he said bluntly. 'With the son of a sheikh. Apparently she'd been planning it since her husband died. Maybe before. Who knows?'

'I'm sorry.'

'*You're* sorry?' He stared at her as if she were part of her sister. They looked alike, Lily thought numbly, and he wasn't seeing her. He was seeing Mia, and the way he felt about her was dreadfully apparent.

There was a long drawn-out silence.

She forced her mind back to the first time she'd met him. He'd been here—reluctantly, she gathered—for the King's celebration of forty years of rule. Not knowing the celebrations were underway, shocked by what the doctors were telling her, she'd been frightened enough to try and visit her sister. She'd been stupid enough to hope Mia would care.

Mia hadn't even wanted to listen. *'Lily, please, this is a very important evening. Everyone else is here to party. Here's a dress. Enjoy yourself. I can't listen to your problems tonight.'*

So she'd sat numbly on the edge of the celebrations, trying not to stare into the chasm of her future. But then Alex had smiled at her and he'd asked her to dance.

And here was the result. Michales. Thought by the world to be Queen Mia's child. Thought, therefore, to be the new King.

No, she thought numbly. Whatever Mia had told the islanders, it was a lie. The true heir was Alex—looking splendid, looking royal, playing his part with ease.

'Have you talked to Mia?' he demanded.

She shook her head. 'That's…that's why I'm here. But I gather she's left…'

'A mess,' he snapped. 'This baby stands to inherit the throne. I'm left in the role of caretaker but I've no power. And here you come… You have no right to be here.'

'I accepted an invitation. I have every right to be here.' She met his gaze calmly, or as calmly as she could manage. Surface calm. Underneath she was jelly.

But somehow she had to break through his anger. She wasn't her sister. He had to see that. 'Alex, last time we met…' she started but his look would have frozen braver souls than her.

'Forget it,' he snapped. 'I don't know what game you were playing…'

'I wasn't playing a game. I was…'

'It doesn't matter.' His anger slashed the stillness. 'What matters now is the future of these islands, and that's nothing to do with you. There are bigger issues. The islanders are enraged. Giorgos and Mia have bled the place dry. I can do nothing to help and I'm stuck with this baby.'

I'm stuck with this baby…

She hadn't known what power he had to hurt her until this moment. Something inside her died, right then.

He was Michales's father. *I'm stuck with this baby...*

It didn't matter. She had to get the baby away.

'So...so what happens now?' she whispered.

'I try and figure a way out of this mess,' he said wearily, as if repeating a tale he was tired of telling. 'The easiest thing to do would be to walk away, but if I do the monarchy will crumble. That'd be a disaster. Giorgos has borrowed to the hilt and most of the island is forfeit if we default. As Prince Regent, I can try and get the economy on its feet. I can service those loans and try to get the land titles back.'

'You can do that?'

'I can try,' he said grimly. 'Do I have a choice?'

'You'd rather be King,' she said and received another flash of anger.

'What do you think?' he demanded. 'I'd like to be King like Giorgos was King? Oh, I'd like his powers. If I was King or Crown Prince instead of Prince Regent, I could restructure the loans and sell royal assets overseas. Did you know Giorgos has properties in Paris, in New York, in London? All over the world. Sold, they'd be worth billions. They'd keep the islanders safe, but as Regent my hands are tied. And your presence helps nothing. Go home, Lily. I don't need another problem.'

'But what happens to Michales?'

'He'll be cared for. Please leave.'

Dear God...

How could she explain things to him when he looked at her as he did now? And would explanations help? If he knew the truth and still made her leave...

She daren't risk it.

Confused, she gazed again at the sleeping baby. That this tiny bundle of perfection could be the result of loving this man...

There was no tenderness now. Alex's voice was implacable. 'Go away, Lily,' he said again, his voice lowering to a growled threat. 'With the way the islanders are feeling, if you show yourself outside these grounds you'll be lucky to avoid being horsewhipped.'

'I'm not to blame for what Mia's done.'

'You're her sister. I have to think you know her better than we do.'

'I hardly know her,' she whispered, touching the soft baby cheek again. There were so many conflicting emotions playing here. 'Alexandros…'

'I don't think you understand. There is no discussion. You need to leave.' His face was stern. Impersonal.

The man she'd once thought she loved had disappeared.

But what was at stake here wasn't a relationship. It couldn't be. What was at stake was *her baby*. The passion she'd once felt for Alex had to be put aside. It was a memory only, she told herself. It had no basis in fact.

'I want a say in how Michales is raised.' Good, she thought. She'd said it. Maybe in time she'd even manage to tell him the truth. Only not now. Not today, when she felt weak and bereft and torn.

'It's up to your sister to agree to your access,' Alexandros told her. 'If she takes back the role of mother, then of course you can take on the role of aunt.'

'I want more.'

'You can't have more. My people have been betrayed by what your sister has done.'

'So they hate me?'

'They don't know you. But you look like her. So no, you can't have access. Contact your sister instead. Drum some sense into her. Make her be a mother.'

'And meanwhile…' she swallowed '…will you be a father to Michales?'

'Are you joking?' He shook his head in disbelief. 'I didn't like his father and I can't abide his mother. I'll make sure there are good people raising him, but he's nothing to do with me.'

'So he'll be raised how you were raised?'

'How the hell do you know how I was raised?'

'You told me, Alex,' she said flatly and he stared at her.

'I must have,' he conceded at last. 'That one night…I hardly remember.'

It needed only that. A night that had changed her world, and he hardly remembered.

'Look, what is this?' he demanded. 'Lily, we slept together but you left the next morning without even a goodbye. Why bring it up again now? I have to think you got what you wanted.' He sighed again, looking weary of the whole business. Weary of her. 'I'll see you get reports of the baby's progress—even though your sister says she doesn't want anything to do with him. That's all I can do.'

'But he's your…'

She couldn't say it. A maid was standing in the doorway, looking anxious. Looking at Lily in recognition.

'Your Highness, you're wanted downstairs,' the girl said to Alex, but she was still staring at Lily. 'I remember you,' she said. 'You're the Queen's sister.'

'I know I'm wanted,' Alex said grimly. 'I was just saying goodbye to Miss McLachlan.'

'Are you leaving, miss?' the girl asked, looking confused.

'I suppose I am,' Lily said, fighting back tears. 'But… I need to spend some time with Michales. Just a little.'

'Take as much time as you want,' Alex agreed, his tone once again implacable. 'Cradle him all night if you want. See if you can make up for his lack of mothering. But you'll stay out of sight of my guests, and you'll leave by tomorrow morning. Goodbye, Lily. Get off my island. You can return with your sister or not at all.'

And, without another word, he wheeled and walked out of the room, leaving her staring after him.

Feeling ill.

'Did someone give you the letter?' the maid asked tentatively across the silence.

'Letter?'

'The Queen…your sister left only yesterday.' There was awe in the girl's voice, as if she still couldn't believe such scandal. 'She told me you were expected.' She crossed to the vast marble fireplace and lifted an envelope from the mantel. 'I promised I'd give it to you. Oh, but, miss, what was she thinking? To abandon her baby…'

Lily closed her eyes, not even thinking how she could answer. When she opened them the girl was gone. Leaving her with the letter.

What have you done, Mia? she asked herself. Dear God, what a mess.

She flicked open the letter and made herself read. It was like Mia. Blunt, with no emotion.

Dear Lily,

I never wanted your baby. Giorgos was so desperate to stop Alexandros inheriting he decided to adopt a child and swear it was ours. He had it set up—bribing doctors— the works. Then, when you told me you were pregnant and too ill to care for the kid, it was like it was meant.

But now Giorgos is dead. I'm no dowager, Lily, asking for pin money from Alex for the rest of my life. Ben's rich and fabulous and I'm going with him. Now your head's been fixed, the baby will be safe with you.

Mia

Lily stared at the letter for so long her eyes blurred. The

blurring was frightening all by itself. The last twelve months
had been blurred and more blurred, and then completely blank.

That Alex could look at her as he had…

Once there'd been tenderness but, as he'd said, it had been
one night of passion, and one night only. It had been a night of
fantasy. Not real.

Her baby was real.

She stared down into the cot and she felt her heart twist.
After all the horror, the bleakness that had been her life thus
far, this was reality. This tiny being.

She'd thought he was the result of loving.

He was. She thought that fiercely. Even though they'd only
just met, she knew she'd loved his father when she'd conceived
this child. Yes, she'd been half crazy with fear, but she'd also
been in love.

Her baby would be loved.

What had Alex said? *Take as much time as you want.*

The door opened and the maid was there again. 'If you
please, miss,' she said. 'It's time for the baby's feed.'

'He's asleep.'

'It's four hours since he was last fed,' the girl said primly.
'We follow rules.'

'I see,' Lily said, swallowing a lump that felt the size of a
golf ball. And then she thought, no. No and no and no.

'You heard what Prince Alexandros said,' she told the girl,
her thoughts eddying and surging, then, like a whirlpool, finding a centre. Enabling her to pull herself together and fight for
what she most wanted. 'Prince Alex said I can take care of
Michales until I leave,' she said. 'Can you bring me his formula—everything he needs until morning—and let us be?'

'What—everything?' the girl said, startled.

'I mean everything.'

'But…we have shifts. We change every eight hours. You
can't look after the baby yourself.'

'Of course I can. A baby should have one carer.'

'The rules…'

'Can start tomorrow,' Lily said flatly. 'For today I'm his aunt and I'm caring for him. I'll feed him and then I'll take him for a walk in the grounds. I'll sleep in here with him tonight. Can you let the rest of the staff know I don't need their help until morning?'

'They won't be happy,' the girl said, dubious.

'Their job is to follow rules,' Lily said softly and she gazed out of the window again, but this time she looked towards the sea, where her borrowed boat lay at anchor, gently rising and falling on the swell of the incoming tide.

Dared she?

How could she not?

This boat wasn't big enough for the journey she had in mind. She'd need help. But then, maybe it was time she called in some favours. What had Mia said? *Ben's rich…*

Her sister owed her big time. That debt was being called in, right now.

'You heard Prince Alexandros,' she said. 'I need to leave. Tomorrow the nursery's yours again, but for today…he's mine.'

It was well into the small hours before Alex found his bed, but still he woke at dawn. He lay staring up at the ceiling, searching for answers.

Trying not to think about Lily.

Thinking about Lily was the way of madness. His life was complicated enough already. He had to find an escape.

There wasn't one. He was locked into a monarchy so out of date that the country couldn't go forward.

And Lily was here.

His head was full already without her. Hell, he had responsibilities everywhere. He was trapped.

But right now all he could think of was Lily. White-faced,

big-eyed, thinner than when he'd last seen her. Flinching as he'd said he couldn't remember their lovemaking.

Maybe he'd been too harsh. Telling her she had to leave.

He had no choice. The islanders were appalled at how her sister had behaved. Lily was, at least outwardly, a less groomed, less glitzy version of Mia. Her clothes were built for practicality rather than glamour, but the islanders would still see her sister in her. She wouldn't be tolerated.

For years the islanders had dreamed that with Giorgos's death they'd be able to purchase their homes, their olive groves, their right to moor their fishing boats without paying the exorbitant mooring rents they'd been charged for ever. But with the birth of Michales their hopes had been dashed. And now… For Giorgos to die and for his Queen to walk away leaving such a legacy…

He didn't blame the islanders for their anger. Rebellion was very close but that'd be a disaster, too. He had to find some way through this mess.

To blame Lily wasn't fair. He knew that. But then, he thought wryly, life wasn't fair. He had no choice but to be here, and Lily had no choice but to leave.

Today.

A knock sounded on his door. He hated the servants intruding—in truth he hated the idea of servants—but he had to grow accustomed.

'Yes?'

'If you please, Your Highness…' It was one of the nursery maids, wide-eyed and big with news.

'Yes?'

'The baby's gone,' she breathed. 'I just put my head around the nursery door and he's gone. And so has Miss Lily. The groundsmen say her boat's no longer anchored in the cove. She's taken our baby, sir. She's taken the Crown Prince.'

CHAPTER THREE

IT WAS six long weeks before he found her.

Alex told the islanders he'd given permission for Lily to care for her nephew while Mia decided what to do, but it was a lie. In reality he had a sworn-to-secrecy team working round the clock, making discreet enquiries, searching across the globe.

Finally his enquiries brought up a birth, registered in the United States:

Michales McLachlan, aged five months, son of Lily McLachlan. Reason for not immediately registering the birth: abroad at time of birth and illness after confinement. Father not listed.

She was registering Michales as hers—as a US citizen. Did she think she could get away with it? He was astounded—furious—and, above all, confused.

Was this a ruse so Mia could get her baby back? It didn't make sense. If Mia wanted him she could have taken him. Yes, Michales was the future King of the Diamond Isles, but that wouldn't have prevented him from being raised overseas.

He had to stop it. The one hope the people of the Diamond Isles held was that this baby was a new start. As Prince Regent,

Alex could ensure this child was raised with a social conscience. Things could get better.

But things couldn't get better if the baby wasn't on the
island where he could influence his upbring.

What the hell was Lily doing? Where was she? And where
was the baby?

Mia and her new consort were in Dubai, living the high life.

Lily and Michales were nowhere.

And then he had a call from one of his…researchers.

'Don't ask me how I know, but she's returning to the States
by boat,' the man told him. 'The *Nahid* belongs to a corpora-
tion owned by Ben Merhdad, the guy Queen Mia's living with.
It's due to dock in Maine on Saturday.'

So here he was, in Maine, on the dock, with two of his men
plus an immigration official he'd briefed. It'd solve everything if this baby was never permitted legal entry to the
United States.

Two minutes before its designated arrival, a magnificent
yacht nosed its way into the harbour.

To his astonishment, Lily was making no attempt to hide.
She was standing on deck, wearing faded jeans and a plain
white T-shirt. Her hair was wrapped in another crazy scarf—a
silk confection. Gorgeous.

She was holding a baby.

There was an audible gasp from the guys around him. 'She's
not even hiding him,' someone said.

'She's registered the baby as hers,' the immigration official
said uneasily. 'She must think she can get away with it.'

'What the hell's she playing at?' Alex growled.

She'd seen him now. Incredibly, she gave him a cheery smile
and a wave. She looked like a woman who'd just returned from
a pleasure cruise.

She looked…lovely.

Or not. He gave himself a sharp mental swipe to the side of

the head. Remember this woman's like her sister. Lovely is surface deep, he told himself. What's inside is selfish, greedy and shallow.

Testosterone was not what was needed.

What was needed was a swift end to this farce.

But she didn't look concerned. She seemed to be the only passenger, standing calmly on the deck as lines were secured...as a crewman carried a couple of bags from below...as Alex gave up waiting and stepped over onto the deck.

'Hi,' she said, and she smiled brightly again, as if he was a friend she was pleased to meet after a casual morning's cruise. 'I thought you might be here. Good detective work.'

'Are you out of your mind?'

'No,' she said, and kept right on smiling. 'Why would you think that?'

'You've taken the baby...'

'No,' she said, and her smile slipped a little. 'Not *the* baby. *My* baby.'

'*Yours.*' The word sucked air from his lungs.

'Michales is mine,' she said. She turned to the crew and her smile returned. 'Thanks, guys. You've been fabulous. Please thank Ben for me. I can manage from here.'

'We've organised transport. And security.' One of the crew— by his demeanour, Alex assumed he was captain—motioned to the dock, and for the first time Alex was aware of a limousine. A uniformed chauffeur was standing at attention, and two dark-suited men stood behind.

'Will I need security?' Lily asked, seemingly of the world at large. 'I'm sure I won't.' She turned back to Alex and gave him another of her bright smiles. 'It's up to you, Your Highness. Will I need muscle to protect what's mine?'

'I don't know what you mean.'

She motioned to the men beside him. 'I think you do. You thought you might take my baby away from me.'

'He's not your baby.'

'He is.'

'Miss.' It was the immigration official. Alex had laid the situation before the US immigration authorities, asking for discretion. This man was senior enough to know what to do, and he had the authority to do it. He was wearing a look of determination and gravitas—an official about to lay down the law. 'According to His Highness, this baby is the Crown Prince of the Diamond Isles. He's the son of King Giorgos and Queen Mia.'

'That was a mistake,' Lily said. 'Michales is mine. His birth is registered under my name. He's a citizen of the United States.'

'That's not been proven,' the man said, clearly unimpressed. 'You can't arrive in the States with a baby and claim he's yours.'

'Without proof,' Lily finished for him.

'Registering the baby's birth isn't proof.'

'No,' she said softly. 'But this is.' She handed over a wallet she'd had tucked under Michales's shawl. 'This is confirmation by legitimate medical authorities that I had a baby less than six months ago. You'll see it's indisputable— the French authorities were very thorough when I told them what I needed. Also attached is the report of DNA samples from my son and from me. I'm happy to have the tests repeated here if you wish, but you'll get the same answers. This baby was passed off by my brother-in-law, the King of the Diamond Isles, as his own, in order to prevent Prince Alexandros ascending to the throne. But this baby is mine, and I intend to keep him.'

She wanted this to be over. She was desperate for it to be over. She needed to sound brave, but inside she felt ill. And the way Alex was looking at her…

No. Concentrate on the official. He was the man she had to convince.

She met the immigration official's gaze directly, trying desperately to ignore Alex. The effect he had on her had to be ignored. Everything about him had to be ignored. 'Is there anything more you need from me?' she managed. 'Michales is due for a feed in less than an hour. I want my son settled in his new home by then. If you gentlemen will excuse us, we need to get on.'

The immigration official was leafing swiftly through the papers, his brow creasing in confused recognition.

'These are highly reputable authorities,' he said at last.

'I told you. I've used the best. But of course, as I said, I'm happy for the tests to be repeated.'

'We'll contact you,' the immigration official said, but his tone had changed. 'In view of this gentleman's allegations…' He motioned to Alex, but there was no way Lily was looking there. 'We may well need to have these verified. But on the surface everything appears in order. Welcome home, miss, to you and your son.'

'Thank you.' It was over. Thank God. She took a step towards the gangplank.

Alex was suddenly in front of her.

On the dock, the two men were out from behind the car almost before he blocked her passage, moving purposely towards them. Good old Ben, Lily thought appreciatively. She'd never met her sister's lover, but in the first flush of romance anything was possible. Especially if you had billions and your girlfriend was being threatened with being landed with an unwanted baby if he didn't agree.

She hadn't meant her threats but she'd used them anyway. 'He's your baby until proven otherwise,' she'd told Mia. 'I'll bring him to you and I'll keep on bringing him to you until you help me.'

So Ben's money was at her disposal. She might need it still, she thought. Alex surely couldn't carry her baby off by force but…who knew? He looked angry enough to try.

'Let me pass, Alex,' she said, but his hands fell onto her shoulders and held.

'What the hell are you playing at?'

'I'm taking what's mine,' she said, jutting out her chin. Trying to sound braver than she was. 'Michales is mine.'

'Are you kidding? He belongs to Mia and Giorgos.'

'I just explained that was a lie.' She took a deep breath. Okay. This had to be said some time. What better time than right now? 'Think about why they might have lied, Alex,' she said gently. 'You'll see for yourself what's happened.'

His anger was building. 'The three of you lied? You agreed to it?'

'I was…ill.'

'You mean you were paid,' he snapped, staring around at the luxury yacht as if it had a bad smell. 'I know your family. You don't have a penny to bless yourself with.'

'Let's not get personal.'

'This is nonsense.' He stared down at the baby in her arms. Cocooned in a soft cream alpaca shawl, Michales slept on, oblivious to the drama being played out around him. 'Of course the baby's Mia's,' he snapped. 'He looks like Mia, and he looks like Giorgos.'

'No, he doesn't,' she said, so softly that no one but Alex could hear.

'He does.'

'Well, maybe a bit,' she conceded. 'But then Mia looks like me. And Giorgos… Giorgos had the Sappheiros royal family features. Who else do I know who might have those features? Work out the dates, Alex. Go figure.'

And, with a faint smile, the result of sheer willpower, she pushed past him.

And that was it. A moment later she was in the limousine. Her baggage was in the trunk and they were moving away.

Alex didn't make a move to follow. He simply stood on the yacht in the warm sunshine and stared after her.

It was done, she thought, shaking with reaction. She'd reclaimed her son.

She could get on with her life.

For days Lily held her breath. She didn't think there was a danger that Alex would try to take Michales forcibly—but she didn't know for sure.

She'd half expected a media frenzy. By reclaiming Michales she was changing the succession of three royal families. The kingdom would dissolve, and the old principalities would take their place. From what she'd figured from reading a potted history of the Isles on the Internet, Alex would now be Crown Prince of Sappheiros. He'd be the real ruler of one island, rather than the caretaker of three.

But it seemed that whatever Alex planned, he wasn't making it public. He hadn't publicised Michales's disappearance either, even though an international hunt might well have blown her cover.

His silence unnerved her, but at least it gave her time to get to know her son. To fall more deeply in love than she'd ever thought she could be.

'It's not the living arrangements you're used to,' she told her tiny son as she introduced him to his new home. Her window looked out over the boatyard. Her boss and his team were at work right under her window, stretching timbers over the frame of a skiff.

She'd soon be down there. The knowledge settled her. Spiros wanted her back and she wanted to be there. If she left her window open she could hear Michales cry, and Spiros's wife would be only too delighted to help.

This could work.

Meanwhile she sat on her faded quilt on her saggy bed and cuddled her son.

She could make him smile, and she was well enough to enjoy him. Life stretched before her, full of endless possibilities. Surely there could be no greater happiness?

Her only cloud? Alex would come, she knew this wasn't over.

Alex—oh, if things could only be different.

They couldn't be different. She forced herself to relax. She forced herself to be optimistic, for there was no going back. This might be Alex's baby, but first and foremost he was hers.

It had taken Alex almost a week to sort things out in his head. Even then they didn't feel sorted. Where to go to from here? He couldn't simply take what Lily told him at face value, tell the islanders they'd been conned and move forward.

But at last, finally, he was starting to accept what she'd told him as the truth.

For the test results Lily had given the immigration official were watertight. Alex had stood by the man's side as he'd rung the French authorities, and he'd heard the outrage that their tests be questioned. Lily had gone to enormous trouble to ensure these were seen as legitimate. She'd organised independent witnesses as DNA samples had been taken. She'd even agreed to have witnesses as she'd been examined to prove she'd borne a child five months ago.

Michales was her baby.

And…*his*? Was she serious?

He remembered the little boy as he'd last seen him, sleeping in his mother's arms. Dark lashes. Thick black curls. Smiling even in sleep.

He was beautiful.

He was his son.

It was too big to take in.

But, believe it or not, this baby was proven to be not the natural child of Mia and Giorgos. There'd been no official adoption—only deception.

The legal ramifications were mind-blowing.

He'd needed help. He'd needed the best constitutional lawyers money could buy, and the best political advisors. He'd consulted them—they'd pored over ancient documents, they'd scratched their heads and they'd outlined facts he didn't want to know.

This was impossible. He needed a magic wand so the past few months could disappear and he could rule without the encumbrance of a baby.

His son.

The more he thought of the lie that had been perpetrated, the sicker he became. That Giorgos and Mia had deliberately deceived the islanders... That Lily had consented...

Had she deliberately seduced him? It had to be faced. Had it been a deliberate plan by the three of them, with Mia pulling out after Giorgos's death only when she'd realised she had no financial independence?

Was Mia's abandonment why Lily had changed her mind and taken her baby back? And what was this illness she'd talked about? She'd been fine six weeks ago at his coronation.

Enquiries to the doctors she'd cited had been stonewalled, citing privacy. Privacy with the succession at stake? Hell, he was almost up to bribing hospital officials to get the answers he wanted.

Not quite. Not yet. He'd ask her directly first.

He'd talked on, privately, to lawyer after lawyer, to advisor after advisor. He'd talked to Stefanos and to Nikos.

He'd thought of one disaster after another...

And when they'd told him the only path that was sure to save the islands he'd felt ill.

Finally, bleak and still unbelieving, he returned to the dockyards, to the address Lily had given the authorities as her permanent home. To the apartment over the boatyard he'd visited once before.

He went alone, slipping in the back way, not wanting to be noticed. Hoping like hell that Lily had rid herself of the bodyguards she'd had with her the week before.

He knocked at the door to her first-floor apartment and he thought this must be a mistake—she'd never live like this. Not Mia's sister.

No one answered. He twisted the doorknob, expecting it to be locked.

It gave under his hand.

Her apartment was one room, simply furnished. There was a double bed, big and saggy, covered with a patchwork quilt that had seen better days. There was a tiny table with a single kitchen chair, a battered armchair, a tiny television, a rod and curtain in the corner constituting a wardrobe.

There was a cot beside the open window. With… With…

Michales? Alone?

No. Ignore the cot. He didn't have space in his head to look at the little person in the cot.

Would he ever?

What sort of a mother was she to leave him alone? Anyone could walk in here.

She was just like Mia.

Concentrate on other things, he thought fiercely. He needed some sort of handle on Lily. Some awareness of who she was.

The apartment was furnished as if the owner had no money to spare, but it didn't scream poverty. Gingham curtains framed the windows. The windows were open, letting in sunlight and the sounds from the boatyard below. There were pots of petunias on the windowsills, and a seagull was balancing on one leg looking hopefully inside.

It looked…great.

It also looked about as far from a royal residence as it could get.

Where was Lily?

Michales…his son…was sound asleep.

His son.

He could just pick him up and take him, he thought. How easy would that be?

What did he want with a baby? With this baby?

With…*his* baby?

He walked over to the window—still carefully not looking at the cot—and glanced out. And there was Lily.

She was right below him, deep in the hull of an embryonic boat. The boat's ribs stretched around her, bare, raw timber. The guy he'd met twelve months before—Lily's boss?—was hauling a length of wood from a steaming vat.

To his amazement, it was Lily calling the shots. She was dressed in serviceable bib-and-brace overalls, workmanlike boots, a baseball cap and thick leather gloves to her elbows. She received the timber from Spiros and her orders flew, curt and incisive.

Her whole attention was on the plank. They had it in place and she was hauling it by hand, pushing, twisting… Two other men were helping, using their brute strength to help her, but Lily was doing the guiding.

He watched on, fascinated. Only when the wood was a fully formed rib, one of the vast timbers forming the skeleton of the new hull, did she stand back and look at it as a whole.

'That's fantastic,' she called. 'Ten down and a hundred and sixty to go? We'll get them done by teatime.'

There was laughter and a communal groan.

She laughed with them. She was…one of the boys? The men were deferring to her with respect.

'I need to check on Michales,' she was saying. 'He's due for a feed. You think you can do the next one without me?' She glanced up at the window.

She saw him.

He'd expected shock. Maybe even fear. Instead, her eye-brows rose, just a fraction. She gave him a curt nod, as if acknowledging past acquaintance, or maybe that she'd attend to him shortly, then deliberately turned her back on him. She strolled over to talk to Spiros.

Spiros was about to lower another plank, but he was looking at it doubtfully. Now he swore and thrust it aside.

'It's not worth it. There's a flaw in the middle and the rest are the same. They'll break before they ever bend. Enough. You go and feed your little one, and I'll send the boys to get more.' He smiled at her with real affection. 'Don't you keep my godson waiting.' Then he, too, glanced up at the window. His smile died.

Spiros stared at Alex for a long minute. What had Lily told him?

Nothing favourable, clearly.

'Hey, look who the cat brought home,' he said, his tone softly threatening. 'It seems we have company.'

His big body was pure aggression. If Spiros had been Lily's father the message couldn't have been clearer. 'You mess with Lily, you mess with me.'

With us. The entire team was gazing at him now. This was hostile territory.

There was a slight noise behind him. He turned and a middle-aged woman was standing in the doorway. Her arms were crossed across her ample breasts. She looked immovable and as aggressive as the men on the docks.

Maybe he couldn't just pick up Michales and take him.

'What do you want?' Spiros demanded from below. 'What the hell are you doing in Lily's apartment?'

'It's okay, Spiros,' Lily said. 'I've been expecting him. Though I shouldn't have left it unlocked.'

'It's okay,' the woman called to Lily. 'I'm here.' She stalked over to the cot and put her body between him and his...the baby.

He couldn't look at...*the baby*.

Unnerved, he looked down at the docks again. Lily was only ten feet under him, giving him a bird's-eye view. She was too thin, he thought. Her bib-and-brace overalls were loose and baggy. Her glorious curls were caught up under a boy's baseball cap, worn back to front. She had a smudge of grease down one cheek.

She looked about fifteen.

But then, 'I'm hoping he's here to organise paternity payments,' she told Spiros, and he stopped thinking of what she looked like.

'He's your baby's father?' Spiros demanded.

'He is. This is Alexandros, Prince Regent of Sappheiros.'

If he'd expected a bit of deference he would have been disappointed. Spiros's aggression simply doubled. Tripled. And the gasp from the woman at the cot was one of indignation and affront.

'So where the hell have you been?' Spiros demanded from below. 'Alexandros of Sappheiros. A prince of the blood, leaving Lily alone with a child... What were you thinking?'

This was crazy. He didn't need these accusations.

He should go down.

Not with the amount of aggression directed at him, he decided. He could talk a lot more reasonably from up here. Especially if he kept his back turned to Madam Fury.

'I searched for her,' he told the boat-builder, trying to keep his voice moderate. Reasonable. 'You know I did.'

'Once,' Spiros said, and spat his disgust. 'You came here once. If she'd been my woman I would have hunted her to the ends of the earth.'

'I'm not his woman,' Lily retorted.

'He's the father of your baby,' Spiros countered, pugnacious. 'Of course you're his woman.'

'Times change,' she said softly. 'You know they do. Spiros, I need to talk to him.'

'Then talk,' he said, glowering. 'Go on. But, prince or no prince, remember he has no rights here. Leave your window open and call us if you need us.' And with a humph of indignation—and a meaningful and warning stare at Alex—he turned his back on him.

CHAPTER FOUR

HE WAS off balance. He shouldn't have entered Lily's apartment. It made him feel like a criminal.

What Spiros had said made him feel like a criminal.

Leaving Lily alone with a child...

How the hell was he supposed to have known?

He heard heavy boots on the stairs. Lily's boots? The door swung open. He turned to face her but she ignored him, making a beeline for the cot.

Michales was still asleep.

Alex waited. He still didn't look at the baby. He couldn't. This was still too big to take in.

Lily though... He could watch Lily. She'd been doing hard manual work. Building boats. He'd heard it before and he'd been hearing verification all week but until now he hadn't believed it.

Mia's sister?

Finally satisfied her son was safe, Lily turned to the woman.

'Thanks, Eleni,' she said. 'I can take it from here.'

Then, as the woman gave him a cold stare and huffed her way out of the door, she turned to him. 'So,' she said, coldly formal, 'what right do you have to walk in here?'

She was angry! There were two sides of that coin.

'I might ask the same of you,' he snapped. 'Entering my palace, stealing the Crown Prince.'

'He's not the Crown Prince and you know it.' She tugged her cap further down over her short-cropped curls. It really was… ridiculous.

'You had no right…' he started, but she crossed her arms over her breasts as Eleni had and glared, lioness guarding her cub.

'I have every right. You can't have him.'

'I'm not saying I want him.'

'No,' she said, and then again, 'no.' Defiance turned suddenly to uncertainty. 'I don't…'

'Know what you want? That makes two of us. Would you mind telling me what the hell is happening?'

'Why should I?'

'For a start, you've implied I'm this baby's father. Am I?'

'Yes,' she said, as if it didn't matter.

It mattered. He'd been working on this, the worst-case scenario, all week, but it still made him feel ill.

Again he couldn't look at the cot. He just…couldn't.

'So you sold him to Giorgos and Mia.'

'I'd never sell him. He's mine, and if you think you're taking him…'

'I'm not here to take him, but I have the right to know what's going on,' he snapped back and she made an almost visible effort to get a hold on her anger.

'Just tell me,' he said. 'You owe me an explanation.'

'I owe you nothing,' she flashed, and then closed her eyes. 'Okay,' she said at last. 'Not that you deserve an explanation, but here goes. I met you, I slept with you and I got pregnant. But I couldn't care for Michales so Mia took him. She and Giorgos told the world he was theirs. I thought they were adopting him. They didn't even do that, which has made my task of reclaiming him a whole lot easier.'

'You're saying you didn't even check what they were doing?'

'That's right,' she said flatly, not even bothering to be defensive. 'I was ill during the pregnancy and I trusted Mia to care for him. I was a fool. Take it or leave it. It's the truth.'

He couldn't believe it. It didn't make sense. 'Mia told the world she was pregnant months before Michales was born.'

'Did she?' She sounded uninterested.

But he was working things out in his head. 'Mia said she didn't want anyone to know of her pregnancy until she was sure she wouldn't miscarry,' he said slowly. 'By the time it was announced, she was five months gone. She was staying in the most exclusive private hospital she could find—abroad, as far from Sappheiros as she could get. Was that so she could bribe people to say your baby was hers?'

'I don't know. I don't care.'

What the hell…? 'Lily, I've had enough,' he snapped. 'To be party to such a fraud…'

'Am I supposed to explain?'

In the cradle behind her, Michales was stirring. Whimpering. Michales.

He had a son.

He'd known for a week. But he needed more time to take it in. A year or so. More.

And into his jumble of emotions came Lily. She was aggressive and uncooperative. But underneath…

There was a reason he'd fallen for her, he thought. Beneath her anger she looked…vulnerable. And very, very desirable. Despite the overalls and the crazy cap. Despite the steel-toed boots.

She made him feel…

Yeah, that was what had got him into this mess in the first place, he told himself savagely. Leave feelings out of it. Find out facts.

Like why she hadn't told him she was pregnant.

'Did I deserve this?' he asked slowly into the silence. 'That you not tell me you were expecting my child?'

'I tried to tell you.' She sounded tired. Flat.

'I don't believe you.'

'I phoned. Three weeks after we'd…'

'Had sex?' he said crudely and she winced.

'If you like,' she managed. 'Maybe that sums up our connection. Dumb, sordid sex.'

It had been more than that. They both knew it. That was what was messing with his head.

'I tried to find you,' he told her.

'Like I believe that. You only had to ask Mia for my address.'

'I did ask Mia. She told me to leave you alone—she was blunt and aggressive and gave no details. But I did end up here. Spiros has told you. And then you phoned.'

'I did,' she said coldly. 'You can't remember what you said?'

'No. I…'

'If you can't, then I can. It's the sort of conversation that sticks in a girl's mind. You find out you're pregnant. You're sick and confused and scared, but finally you work up courage to contact the baby's father. And his line is… "Lily. Great to hear from you. You're not trying to slap a paternity suit on me as well, I hope."'

He stilled.

He'd said it. God forgive him, he'd said it.

He remembered, all too clearly.

He was a prince, a bachelor, titled and eligible. He'd made a fortune himself, and as Giorgos's heir he stood to inherit much, much more. As such, he'd endured the most blatant attempts to…get close.

The morning Lily had called he'd just fielded a call from the mother of a Hollywood starlet. Vitriolic and accusing.

'You slept with my daughter and now she's pregnant. You'll marry her or you'll pay millions.'

He'd never slept with the girl. He couldn't remember even meeting her. But obviously the girl was pregnant, and she'd named him as the father.

It happened.

And about ten minutes after that, Lily had called.

He *had* slept with Lily. He'd been angry that she'd left, frustrated that he hadn't been able to find her—and, despite his precautions, pregnancy was possible, though unlikely. So he'd come out with his glib, joking line…

'You're not trying to slap a paternity suit on me as well…'

She'd said…what was it? 'Get lost.' And cut the connection.

He remembered staring at the phone, feeling bad, thinking he should trace the call. And then thinking of Mia and how much he disliked her—how much he loathed Lily's connection to royalty. And how much attachment hurt. How love ended in grief. How a sister of Mia's could never be worth that hurt. And it had sounded as if she clearly didn't want him anyway.

And he'd made the conscious decision, there and then, not to make any further attempt to contact her.

'You could have tried again,' he said, but her face was grim now, and drawn.

For over a year now he'd tagged this woman as just like her sister. He'd treated her accordingly. His response to her phone call had been glib and cruel, but if it had been Mia he'd been talking to, maybe it would have been justified.

She wasn't Mia.

And now? She was expecting him to walk away. No, she was wanting him to walk away. With or without paternity payments, he thought. The fact that she wanted nothing to do with him was obvious.

Unbidden, he remembered Lily as he'd first seen her. Dressed simply in a little black dress. Very little make-up. Those glorious curls.

He'd said something sardonic about their surroundings—the glitz of the royal ballroom—and she'd chuckled her agreement. 'I do like a bit of bling,' she'd said. 'Mind, these chandeliers are a disappointment. I'd prefer them in pink. Plain crystal is so yesterday's fashion. Like stove-pipe pants and shoulder pads.' She'd eyed him up and down—in his tuxedo. 'And tuxedos,' she'd said, and she'd said it like a challenge.

He'd been entranced.

But there was no trace of that humour now. Her gaze was glacial.

'I don't have to tell you more,' she said. 'You're not King here.'

'I'm not King anywhere.'

'Or Prince Regent.'

'It seems I'm not Prince Regent either,' he told her. 'If Michales isn't Giorgos's son…' He hesitated, trying to find words to clarify what he'd figured over the last week. 'If we can get this sorted without calamity, the Diamond Isles will be split into three again. I'll be Crown Prince of Sappheiros and Khryseis and Argyros will be ruled as separate countries.'

'So can you get this sorted?' she asked, but she didn't sound interested.

'Maybe. No thanks to you.'

'On the contrary, it's all thanks to me,' she snapped. 'If I hadn't claimed Michales you'd still be ruled by my sister's lie. So now you can be whatever sort of prince you want and you can get out of my life.'

'There's the small issue of my son…'

'You need to earn the right to be a father. I've seen no evidence of it.'

'I didn't know he was my son!'

'You've known for a week. So what did you do? You disappeared. You went away and did anything rather than come here and say *this is my son and I want him*.'

'I didn't know…' he started, but then he paused, unsure where to go.

'You didn't know what?'

'I don't know how I'm supposed to feel,' he snapped. 'I needed time.'

'Like I needed time when I saw the thin blue line,' she retorted. 'Parenthood isn't something you can think about and then decide *ooh, maybe I'd like a little bit.*'

'Isn't that exactly what you did?'

'I had no choice.' She moved still closer to the cot, putting her body between him and her baby. It was a gesture of defence as old as time itself.

'So why did you give him up?' he demanded, trying to keep his focus on indignation. Trying not to think how beautiful she was when she was angry. How vulnerable. How…frightened?

'How much did they pay you?'

'Millions!' The word was a venomous hiss.

Okay, not millions, he conceded.

What, then? Had she simply offered her son to her sister instead of having him adopted?

Had she really been ill?

His eyes flew to her baseball cap. She'd covered her curls at the coronation, too.

Cancer? But Lily didn't have that look. Soft curls were escaping from under the cap—short, yes, much shorter than last year, but not regrowth short.

'Just how ill were you?'

'It's none of your business.'

'Your hair…'

'I had an operation,' she snapped. 'I'm fine now.'

He got the message. Ask no more questions. Move on.

Okay, he would. But maybe here there was an explanation.

The consequences of illness, even if relatively mild, might well have been catastrophic. If she didn't have insurance, medical expenses could be huge.

If Mia and Giorgos had paid her expenses and in return taken a child she could ill afford to keep… A child she didn't really want, until Mia's abandonment had given her second thoughts…

It didn't absolve her from blame, but it might explain it.

Maybe something of what he was thinking was apparent.

'Don't even think about pushing into what's my business,' she told him coldly. 'Let's get this sorted. If you want to deny Michales is your son, that's fine by me. I don't need or want financial aid. If you want access I won't block it—as long as he stays with me. But that's my bottom line. He stays with me.'

'I can't let him stay here.'

'He will stay here.' She sounded blunt and cold and definite. But, underneath, he heard the beginnings of fear.

There was no way he could allay that fear.

'I have to take him back to Sappheiros.'

'You're taking him nowhere.'

'Michales has to be my son.'

'So he is,' she snapped. 'Move on.'

'He has to be my legitimate son.'

That confused her. 'Excuse me?'

'Can you imagine the furore there will be if he disappears? The islanders are upset enough now that you've taken him. For you to keep him…'

'He's mine!'

'The islanders think he's theirs.'

'He's not.'

'He is,' he said. 'You and Mia and Giorgos gave him to the island. The islanders have taken him to their hearts. I won't take him away from them.'

'It's not you who's taking him away.' She was whispering but she might as well be yelling, it was said with such vehemence. 'It's me. He's mine, and he stays with me.'

As if on cue, Michales stirred again, uttering a small protesting whimper. She scooped him from his cot and held him against her. He snuggled into her and her fingers stroked his hair.

The sight…watching her stroke the little boy's hair did something to him he didn't begin to recognise.

This was getting harder. He'd come here fuelled with anger against this woman. He'd come here to try and sort a solution.

What he hadn't counted on was how she made him feel. He'd slept with Lily over twelve months ago and his body still knew why. He was reacting to her as he had then—with a desire that was inexplicable but inarguable.

And Michales…

He'd never thought of himself as a father. This child had nothing to do with him.

Except… He had the look of him. *His son.*

His world was shifting into unchartered territory.

Just say it, he told himself again, feeling cornered. Lay it on the line.

'Lily, this is hard,' he said. 'But you need to listen. The islanders have lived with such uncertainty that when the truth comes out about Michales's parentage their likely reaction will be disbelief. And why wouldn't it be? They've been lied to by Mia and Giorgos. They have no reason to trust me—or you.'

'I don't… It can't matter.'

'But it does matter,' he said forcefully. 'We need to give them reason to believe, and the way to do that is by acting truthfully and acting with honour.'

'Honour…' She filled the word with scorn. 'Honour!'

'I know it's been in short supply, but this is my honour,' he said, ruefully now. 'I need to be seen to do the right thing.'

'Finally.'

'Okay, finally,' he admitted and spread his hands in apology. 'I concede my behaviour until now has been less than perfect. I shouldn't have slept with you. I shouldn't have blocked your phone call with such a response. But we…both of us…need to move on. The islanders need to be told that Giorgos and Mia lied, but they need to accept that the lies are finished. They need to know I'm to be trusted—and that I'm truly Michales's father. Right now the island is on the brink of rebellion, but my advisors believe that it would be reluctant. We can head it off by giving the island stability, good government and hope for the future. The island needs an honourable royal family and it needs an heir.'

Lily stared at him over Michales's small head. 'S-so?'

But maybe she was already seeing where he was going, he thought. She looked suddenly terrified. She was a lot smarter than Giorgos, he thought. Or her sister.

'I'm assuming you know the state of the Diamond Isles.'

'Yes, but…'

'But ruin,' he said forcefully. He couldn't let the shock on her face deflect him from what needed to be said. 'The islanders are poverty-stricken. The islands' land titles are mortgaged to the hilt and there's threatened takeover by outside interests. We're facing destruction of our lifestyle—everything we stand for. That's inevitable, unless these people put their faith in me and in what I can do. The islanders have to accept their new royal family—they can't think I'm inventing this story merely to claim the throne for my own ends. Lily, I've thought about this all week. I've listened to the wisest lawyers and political advisors I can find. And they've come up, over and over, with the one sure answer.'

'Which…which is…'

'Which is that you marry me.'

CHAPTER FIVE

FOR a moment he thought she'd faint. The colour bleached from her face. She stared at him in incredulity. Instinctively his hands caught Michales and held.

She was so stunned she let her baby go. He stood, holding his son. Not sure how to hold him. Not sure where to go from here.

'Maybe I didn't do that too well,' he said at last. Then he said dryly, 'Maybe I should go down on bended knee.'

'Or maybe you shouldn't.' Colour washed back, a flush of anger. Better, he thought. Angry was good.

He could deal with anger.

'I think you need to leave,' she said. 'I'm talking about getting on with the rest of my life. You're talking fairy tales.'

'I'm not.'

Michales wriggled in his arms. He looked up at Alex and he smiled, a wide, toothless grin that made Alex feel as if the rug was being pulled from under his feet.

He had to keep hold of his anger. He couldn't think while holding…*his son*.

He laid him on the square of carpet under the window. The little boy pushed himself into a sitting position and crowed with delight.

Alex gazed down at him in astonishment. 'He can almost sit up. He wasn't doing that in Sappheiros.'

'As if you'd have noticed.'

'I did notice,' he told her. 'Even before Mia left I was worrying about him. The nursery staff were worrying about him. His mother seemed to be ignoring him.'

'Yeah,' she said, sounding dazed. 'Alex, go away.'

'I can't,' he said soberly, and instinctively he caught her hands. They were cold. Too cold. She didn't pull away, though—she didn't move.

Okay. Get this right, he told himself. Stay logical and unemotional.

'It's politics,' he told her. 'If we leave things as they are, if he stays here with you, the islands will be in a mess. They'll see me as a usurper, and rebellion is a real possibility. But if we marry…'

She tugged her hands back in instinctive protest, but he didn't let her go. He had to impart the urgency of the situation, and at the same time he was trying to figure how to take the blank look from her face.

She looked…battered. It might be a front, but he needed to back off.

He needed to talk a language they both understood.

'You obviously don't understand,' he said. 'But I'm talking money.'

And here it was. He'd come prepared.

'There's a cheque in my pocket for more money than you can dream of,' he told her. 'Call it paternity payment if you like, but it's yours the moment you marry me.' Then, as she stared at him in stupefaction, he ploughed on. 'This is not personal. Think of it as a business proposition. The proposal is that you marry me—a real wedding to reassure everyone that we stand together—you stay on Sappheiros for at least a year so our marriage can't be annulled, and then we can be seen as gradually drifting apart. Once the island is stable we can divorce. You can do what you want. You'll be rich and you'll be free. I can put democratic reform in place so the Crown is titular head only, and you can do whatever you want for the rest of your life.'

And, before she could respond, he produced the cheque and handed it to her.

She took the cheque without saying a word. She stared at him. She stared down at the cheque—and she gasped.

It'd be okay. Money talked. He had this covered. As long as he married her.

He had no choice.

'This…this is for real?' she whispered.

'Absolutely,' he said. 'We've thought of every option and this is the only one we believe can work.'

She was staring at him as if she'd never seen him before. She was staring at him as if he was a lunatic.

'There's more,' he said into the silence. 'We've done a lot of digging in this last week. My researcher knows all about you and the people you work with and we've come up with a package deal. Apparently the only strong connection you seem to have is with Spiros and his team. We've learnt that Spiros's boatyard is struggling. As an inducement—because it would be best for everyone if Michales does stay on the island, and thus you, too—I'm also offering Spiros something he can't refuse. We'll relocate this boatyard to Sappheiros, with every cost taken care of. We'll give him transport of boats between the Diamond Isles and the rest of Europe. We'll give him blanket international advertising. My researchers tell me Spiros has been fighting to make a living here, and he's homesick. He and his wife want to live somewhere they can speak their native Greek. So all you need to do now is agree.'

She said nothing. She was staring at the cheque as if she couldn't believe it.

She was so shocked. She was so…

Beautiful?

Don't go there, he told himself sharply. This was a business proposition—nothing more, nothing less. His lawyers had worked it out as a done deal. 'There's no way she'll knock back this offer,' he'd been told, and for good measure, thinking of Mia's greed, they'd added another zero to the cheque.

As Crown Prince, Alex would inherit all Giorgos's wealth. The lawyers' thinking was that he should use a fraction of this to ensure the island's future. This marriage of convenience was necessary. Michales's continued presence on the island was desirable. So pay her and get it sorted. But…

'Get out,' she said.

He didn't move.

'Get out.' She was breathing too fast, her eyes flashing daggers. 'How dare you…?'

'Propose marriage to the mother of my son?'

'He's not your son.'

'You said…'

'By birth, yes. You want him back on the island for you? *For you?* Michales hasn't come into this discussion once except as a tool to keep the monarchy safe. Neither have I. For you to manipulate me…to find out about Spiros and use him as a tool… Get out and stay out.'

'Lily, look at the amount on that cheque,' he said urgently. 'You can't possibly knock back what I've just offered.'

'Watch me,' she said and she ripped the cheque in half, in half again and then kept on going until it lay in shreds round her feet. She snatched Michales up and stalked to the door. 'Out!'

'You're being ridiculous. If you want more…'

'*You're* being ridiculous,' she snapped back at him. 'Don't you understand? I have everything I want, right here, right now. I have something you and Mia and people like you can't understand. I have *enough*. I can stay working on the boats I love, and I can raise my son. I have my future and I'm free. Why would I possibly jeopardise that by diving into the royal goldfish bowl?'

Free? How did free come into it? She spoke as if she'd just come out of prison.

He had to make her see sense.

'And Spiros?'

'He's happy here.'

'He's not. Any minute now this business is going to go belly up. Ask him.'

'That's nothing to do with you.'

'It's everything to do with you. You have to marry me.'

'I don't have to marry you.' She opened the door. 'Get out,' she said again.

'I can't,' he said, trying to figure where the hell to take it from here. 'Lily, you have to do this. The islanders are facing ruin. If I don't get this succession sorted, the titles belonging to the Crown will be forfeit to outside business interests. Sappheiros will become an exclusive resort for the rich, and my people will be exiles. The other two islands will face a similar fate.'

Her face stilled. For the first time, she hesitated.

He paused.

Was he going about this the wrong way? Was it possible that this woman had the heart that Mia lacked?

She'd given away her baby. The assumption had been she'd done it for profit, for greed. But now…

She looked pale and sick. And suddenly that was how he was feeling. Sick.

He was starting to feel…smirched. As if he was acting as Mia and Giorgos had acted. Buying her baby. Buying her.

'Get out,' she whispered again, and this time he nodded.

'I'm going. But…' He hesitated but it had to be said. 'Lily, this is too fast. It's urgent but it's not about us. I suspect I've misjudged you, and if I have then I'm sorry.'

'That's kind of you.' She was trying to sound sardonic but her voice was shaking.

She swayed, just a little.

He moved, crossing the few steps to her in an instant, holding her shoulders. Steadying her.

'Don't...don't touch me.'

But she didn't pull away. She couldn't. She was holding on to Michales with one arm, with the other the door handle. 'Please leave.'

Hell, how ill had she been? 'Lily, are you okay?'

'I'm fine,' she managed and steadied. She tugged away and he released her with real regret. She seemed suddenly... frail?

It didn't make sense. Nothing made sense.

He'd walked into this room feeling nothing but anger at the mess this woman had got him into. Determined to act with honour, no matter what the cost. Now, stupidly, all he wanted was to protect her.

It didn't make sense to her either. She was looking at him with a mixture of fear and something else. Something he couldn't pinpoint.

Regret? The word slipped into his mind and stayed.

Regret for what he'd done to her? Regret that she couldn't take up his offer?

Maybe she had used him. Maybe the pregnancy had been planned. But this was...deeper.

He thought of how she'd been little more than a year ago. She'd danced with him, she'd teased him, she'd mocked him and he'd been enchanted. What had happened to knock the spirit from her?

'Lily, I'll leave,' he said and flinched inwardly as he saw relief flood her face. Was she so afraid of him? 'I've come at you too fast, too hard.'

'Yes,' she said blankly.

The pieces of the cheque were still scattered on the floor. There were far too many for her to gather and reassemble after he left.

But she'd seen his glance—and she guessed what he was thinking.

'I won't,' she said, her face flushing with anger again.

'I know you won't.'

'You don't know anything about me.'

He was starting to know more.

From Lily's arms Michales was watching him with interest. *He was his son...*

How could he have been convinced that a simple cheque could fix things? It seemed so ridiculous now.

If Lily hadn't been Mia's sister—if he hadn't assumed this had been set up as a con—what would he have done?

Appeal to a conscience he'd assumed she couldn't have?

If she did have a conscience, there was nothing to lose—and everything to gain.

'Do you have access to the Internet?'

His simple question caught her off guard. 'I...yes...'

'Then I'll leave you. But I need you to do something. I want you to look up the websites of our local newspapers.' He pulled out a card and scribbled addresses on it. 'Then contact these men. They'll give you their own references. What they'll do—I hope—is convince you that what I say is true. The islands are facing ruin. Only my marriage to you can save them.'

'But I don't want to be married. I want to be free.'

'Free?'

'Yes, free.' Her colour suddenly returned in force, surging behind her anger. 'I'm free,' she said, sure now. 'For the first time in my life I can move forward, where I want, when I want. You think I'd go from that to *marriage...*' She said the word as if it were some sort of hell. 'How can you ask it of me? You have no right.'

Was the thought of marriage to him so appalling? It didn't make sense.

He wasn't *that* bad. Was he?

It couldn't matter. All he could do was tell her the facts. 'I have no choice,' he said. 'And if you have a conscience, then you don't either.'

Her anger was palpable. Maybe if she'd had a hand free she'd have slapped him, he thought. Maybe it would have made them both feel better. What was between them needed some release—there was nowhere to go with the rising tension.

'Just contact these people,' he said. 'Ask the questions.'

'Go.'

'I'll come back tomorrow. Lily, we're running out of time and you must take this seriously. Combined, you and I hold the fate of the islands, and Sappheiros in particular, in our hands. Whether we want it or not, we need to be married.'

She looked up at him in bewilderment. Anger was giving way to confusion.

'I'm sorry,' he said simply. 'But we have to do this. And maybe it won't even be too bad.'

And then—maybe it was really dumb but he couldn't not— he lifted Michales from her arms. Once more, he set the little boy on the floor.

He took Lily's face in his hands.

And he kissed her.

It was no deep, demanding kiss. He had enough sense for that— almost. But that night a year ago hadn't been an aberration. His body knew what it wanted—and it wanted her.

The kiss was a feather-touch, lips to lips, sweet as honey, and a connection that felt intrinsically right. It was as if a part of him had reconnected that he hadn't known until this moment had been cut loose.

He kissed her and she didn't respond, but neither did she pull away.

Should he take it further?

His body was telling him to deepen the kiss, push past the barriers he could feel she'd erected.

His head was screaming the opposite. He'd pushed her too far as it was. The royal succession hung on this young woman's decision. To push her past the point where she might run…

He shouldn't. But kissing her felt right. It felt entirely natural. Lily…

And things were changing.

Suddenly it was Lily who was taking control.

He'd outlined a business proposition. So why was he kissing her?

She should fight him. She shouldn't let him kiss her.

She was passive, letting him do the running, letting him kiss her…

Why had she done this? Why had she let him?

She knew why. She just had to see…if what she remembered was real.

Like beer. It was a stupid analogy but she'd thought of it a few times over the past months.

The first time she'd been given a glass of beer, it had been after a day spent working in the hold of a sun-baked boat. She'd been hot to the point of exhaustion. She'd been so thirsty her tongue was swollen, and she remembered that beer as almost like nectar.

The next time she'd tasted beer it had been an ordinary day—no heat, no exhaustion. She remembered being deeply, intensely disappointed.

So now…for all these months she'd been convincing herself that what she felt for Alex had to be a combination of time, place and mood. Nothing more.

But she had to see.

So stupidly, dumbly, she let herself try.

Alex's kiss had been tentative, questioning. She felt the first stirrings of regret. This wasn't as she remembered.

She should pull away while she still felt like this.

But she had to push harder. The memory was still too strong to let her release it without grief. She had to take the next step.

She put her hands on either side of his face, she pulled him closer—and she kissed him back.

And here it was again.

Magic.

She'd fallen for this man hard, and she remembered why. No. She didn't have to remember. It was imprinted on her brain, on her body.

Heat. Aching need. Pure animal magnetism.

The crazy conversation of the last few minutes faded—everything faded, there was only this man and his mouth on hers and his body close to her. His taste, his feel, his masculine scent.

She'd remembered this man during the nightmare of the past few months and she'd thought her memories must be imagination born of illness and of loneliness.

But this was real. This was Alex.

Her Prince. Her man.

She felt her lips open and taste as she'd tasted him before. She was kissing him as fiercely as he was kissing her—and maybe consciousness didn't come into a decision like this.

Maybe it just had to happen.

She let herself sink into the kiss. For this one sweet moment she allowed herself the luxury of believing this passion meant something to him. Her fingers twined through his hair and she tugged him closer. Closer.

For just this minute she could savour him, taste him, hold him. Pretend he was really her man, he was her future and everything would fall into place. She'd have a happy ever after.

Maybe ever-after didn't cut it, she thought numbly. Now was the important thing. Now. Here. Alex.

He made her feel so sexy he took her breath away. Desire started deep within, and built.

She wanted him so much.

Her body was on fire, burning with a heat she'd felt once before with Alex, but never before and never since. She was aching for him, hot for him, moist for him, right here, right now, fully clothed, with the only contact being his mouth on hers.

She was helpless in the face of her body's response. She felt herself shift, move closer, so close she was aching to be a part of him.

He could take her here, right now, she thought wildly, regardless of no protection, of no hope for a future, of nothing but burning want. She'd been ill for so long...hopeless for so long...but, within her now, life was surfacing. *She* was surfacing in her response to this man. A primeval need...

Alex.

His body was magnificent. Unimaginably erotic. He was holding her hard against him. His hands were strong and warm, curving into the small of her back, pressing her breasts against his chest, crushing her to him as if he wanted her as much as she wanted him...

If she could just get nearer...

She was out of control and she didn't care.

She let herself go...

But things had changed since the last time she'd let herself love this man. She had a son. And in the end it was Michales who broke the kiss.

The baby was sitting at their feet, gazing up at the adults above him in some indignation. Michales was unaccustomed to being ignored. He needed a feed. He needed attention.

So he did what any self-respecting baby would do in the circumstances. He opened his mouth and he howled.

Michales.

Her baby.

Reality slammed home. She pulled away from Alex as if

he were burning her. Which pretty much explained how she was feeling.

She lifted Michales, she hugged him against her and she held him tight, as if he were a shield.

She'd been out of control. Again. After all she'd been through. After all her vows. This man just had to touch her and here she was, tumbling into trust again.

Trust meant heartache. Trust meant betrayal and grief.

Do not trust this man.

This had to stop—now.

Had he messed it up entirely?

He'd come here with a business proposition. He'd never imagined he could seduce her into doing what he wanted.

Was that what she was thinking?

Who knew what she was thinking? She looked dazed.

He felt dazed.

He had to get this back on an impersonal footing.

'That's just what we don't want,' he managed.

'Sorry?'

'That wasn't meant to happen. We need to keep this impersonal or we'll mess this up entirely.'

'Right,' she said, as if she didn't understand a word he'd said. Which was exactly how he felt.

'I'll come again tomorrow,' he said, struggling to sound brisk and businesslike. 'Meanwhile, will you do some research? Discover what I've said is true?'

Her face had become…blank? It was as if she'd just terrified herself and was struggling back from the abyss. Struggling to hold on to what she knew.

'I don't know why I did that,' she whispered. 'It was crazy. I didn't mean it. I don't want it. I don't want you to touch me.'

She was lying. They both knew it. But there was fear behind her words. He didn't understand it.

She'd come to him last time with joy. Had being pregnant changed something so fundamental that she was afraid of his effect on her?

'I want my freedom,' she said, a flat statement, unequivocal.

What sort of a need was that?

But freedom was the one thing he was more than prepared to give. After all, wasn't that what he wanted himself?

'You can have it,' he said. 'But marry me first.'

'I can't.'

'I believe you can. For Michales's sake.'

'You…don't want Michales for him. You just want him for your island.'

He hesitated, letting himself look at the little boy who gazed placidly back at him. These were his own eyes?

You just want him for your island.

This was way too complicated.

'It's a business decision,' he said flatly, trying to move on. 'Look, that kiss was an aberration. It has to be. If we let sentiment get in the way it'll never work. I don't want to pressure you but I must. It's not our lives, Lily. It's the fate of an entire country, possible three.'

'Right.'

'It is,' he said. 'Will you think about it?'

'Yes. Just go away.'

Just like that. He had her agreement.

There was nothing else to stay for. Was there?

'If I agree…' she whispered. 'If I was stupid enough to say yes… Could we still be independent? I do not want to fall for you again.'

'Did you fall…?'

'Shut up,' she snapped. 'Fall? Of course I fell. I was an idiot over you. I turned my life into a mess, all because I acted like a lovesick teenager. You kiss me and I turn into that stupid teenager again. If what you say is true…if there really is this huge moral need for me to marry—then we do it as a business deal. Nothing more. I'm not letting you touch me again.'

'I'd rather not…'

'Touch me? Then don't.'

'Lily…'

'Enough,' she snapped. 'I'll think about it. I'll do the homework. And then, if I must, I'll outline conditions. But kissing doesn't come into it.'

'That's a shame,' he said and tried a smile but she glowered.

'Don't you turn that charm on me. I know it. I let you kiss me once to see if what I was afraid of was true, and it is. Now I know where I stand, that's the end of it. If we have to get married then we do exactly what the law requires and nothing more. If I have to do anything that even remotely resembles conjugal rights…'

'Conjugal…' he said cautiously and ventured a smile.

She didn't smile back. 'Enough,' she said. 'Get out. Conjugal or no conjugal, and don't you push me, Alexandros Mykonis—you know exactly what conjugal means.'

'Right.'

She was glowering at him. She'd promised to think about it. There was nothing to be gained by staying.

He'd got what he wanted.

Hadn't he?

She heard his steps fade to nothing. She closed the door and leaned on it, and her whole body shook.

Marriage. Alex.

No and no and no.

Marriage to almost any other man wouldn't be as bad. Because marriage to Alex…it'd be surrender.

He'd kissed her and she'd surrendered, just as she'd surrendered a year ago. Had she learned nothing?

Alex.

She'd have to do the research.

If she was Mia she'd just walk away.

'I want to be Mia,' she whispered, but she knew it wasn't true.

She wanted…she wanted…

Life.

Her body wanted Alex.

She crossed to the window and looked out. He hadn't gone far. He was just below her window, talking to Spiros.

Was he making her boss this crazy proposition already? To relocate Spiros's boatyard to Sappheiros?

Spiros would love it. He and Eleni had come to this country because Spiros dreamed of making his living building the boats he loved, but if he thought he could do it on Sappheiros he'd be there in a minute.

It could happen—if she said yes.

If she promised to marry Alex.

She wanted to lean out of the window, yell at them that this was some crazy proposition by a madman. It was emotional blackmail. She had the right to walk away.

When had she ever had a choice?

She sank onto the floor with Michales and hugged her knees. She felt very tired, alone and afraid.

Alex had kissed her.

And that was what she was most afraid of. He exposed her for what she was. Vulnerable and wanting.

'Love's crazy,' she said. Then, as Michales looked seriously at her, she tugged him onto her knees. 'It only causes trouble. It caused…you.'

Her son would be heir to the throne of Sappheiros. He'd be the legitimate heir, following in his father's footsteps.

It was unbelievable. It was…terrifying.

She rose again and went back to the window. Alex was still there. Spiros was smiling—more than smiling. He was looking incredulous. He was glancing up at her window and she drew back into the shadows.

This was worse than blackmail. He'd placed the islanders' fate in her hands. He'd placed Spiros's fate in her hands.

What if it was a lie? In this day and age, for a marriage of convenience to be the only path to prevent disaster… It was inconceivable.

But she'd promised to do the research, and if it was true…

This was like jumping off a cliff and not knowing what was below. Only knowing that, whatever was at the end, by the time she landed she'd be going so fast the force could kill her.

CHAPTER SIX

Sappheiros Times headlines

14th August:

> 'Royal Scandal—Secret Baby'
> 'Queen Uses Sister's Baby to Keep Throne'

16th August:

> 'After the Lies, Prince Regent Is Ruling Crown Prince'

21st August:

> 'Islands Revert to Ancient Lineage'
> 'Three Principalities From One Kingdom: Islanders' Joy'

23rd August:

> 'DNA Proves Baby Still Heir! Alexandros Confesses Affair'
> 'Prince to Wed Queen's Sister'
> 'Prince Declares Lily a Worthy Princess'
> 'Wedding By End of Month'

* * *

Two weeks. It was only two weeks since she'd been hit with this crazy proposition and it had moved from crazy to terrifying. She was standing at the entrance to the cathedral, ready to be a bride.

Was she out of her mind?

Maybe she was, but she'd done the research. Everything she'd read confirmed and reconfirmed what Alex had told her. Giorgos and his forebears had brought the Diamond Isles to ruin. The only way they could be saved was for them to revert to their original states; for their original ruling families to take their care into their hands. But there was such distrust...

She'd looked at it from every conceivable angle and there was no escape. From the moment she'd seen Spiros's face, full of incredulous hope, she'd known what she had to do.

Alex had come back the next day and she had her answer ready.

'Yes,' she'd told him. 'For a year. No more. And you touch me and the deal is off. It's a marriage in name only. Is that clear?'

'It's what I want,' he'd told her. Then, watching her, clearly unable to figure out her response, he'd added, 'It's a marriage, Lily. It's not the gallows you're walking into.'

'It's a trap,' she'd said. 'I'm doing it but I don't have to like it.'

'It's not a trap of my setting and I don't like it either,' he'd said.

And then he'd left. There was financial chaos in Sappheiros, he'd told her, and he had to sort it out. But the wedding was to take place by the end of the month.

And then the roller coaster began. Or the avalanche. Or whatever it was, but it made her so giddy she thought surely she must still be drifting in and out of the same nightmare world she'd been in before.

Arrangements, arrangements, arrangements. Curt, formal telephone calls with Alex, interspersed by longer calls from officialdom, arranging everything from her bridal gown to a white teething ring for Michales so he could chew his gummy way through the ceremony and still look…bridal?

Yes, the thing was ridiculous, and finally she decided okay, if it was ridiculous she'd simply treat it as a joke gone wrong. She'd close her eyes and get it over with.

And here she was. Her wedding day.

She was about to enter the cathedral where Alexandros had taken his vows two months before. The last time she'd entered this cathedral, she'd slipped in at the rear, wanting to remain anonymous.

Now… Every man and woman was on their feet, waiting for her entrance, and Alex was standing at the altar. The Archbishop was in front and central. Waiting for her.

She was ready to walk down the aisle. Alone.

'Have Spiros give you away,' Alex had told her. 'You can't do this by yourself. Stefanos and Nikos will attend me. You need bridesmaids. At least have Spiros.'

'I need no one,' she'd said. 'I don't see why we can't do this in a government office.'

'It needs to be done with all the pomp and splendour we can muster,' he'd told her. 'The islanders need reassurance that this is real—no one should disbelieve that you're my wife.'

'I'm not your wife.'

'You are,' he'd said gravely. 'You've agreed.'

'Until you have the island stable. No more.'

'Then for the time we have I'll do you honour.' In a different tone this might have been a lovely thing to say but it was said in the tone of a man who knew where his duty lay. 'As the country will do you honour and as you'll do yourself honour. It's meant as a reassurance to the country that we can move forward. There'll be nothing secret or covert about it. You'll wear full royal regalia, as will I.'

This final decree had left her almost speechless. 'A real

royal wedding?' She hadn't attended Mia's wedding—they'd been so distant by then that Mia would never have thought of inviting her—but she'd seen the media coverage and the thought of doing the same left her cold. 'You're telling me what I should wear?'

'My people tell me there's no time to make you a completely new gown but if you'll agree… The royal wedding gowns have been amazing over the centuries, and they've been carefully stored and kept, every one. If we can get you here a few days before the wedding, we can get one altered. You could even wear Mia's.'

And then he'd listened to the silence and conceded, 'Okay, maybe not Mia's. But there will be one that fits you. There's no time to make you one as splendid, and this has to be done right.'

Fine. She was past arguing.

She could do it.

She'd flown here four days ago. The royal assembly line had swung into place the minute she'd arrived. She'd been shown to her own apartment within the palace—an apartment she assumed would be hers for the duration of her marriage. It was opulent to the point of crazy. They'd suggested Michales use the royal nursery and she'd knocked that on the head. There was a cot in the corner of her apartment now; as long as she had Michales she could live anywhere.

So she'd done what was expected, whatever she was told. She'd hardly seen Alexandros and then only when he'd been surrounded by palace officials, lawyers, advisors.

She'd been given her own lawyers. That had surprised her. In all the chaos she'd been given this one sliver of control. The lawyers had been engaged in her name, and they'd been competent and thorough in drawing up a pre-nuptial agreement for her protection. She had no doubt that at the end of her marriage she could walk away—with Michales and with an allowance that made her head swim.

She'd put up a feeble protest about the money but her lawyers had simply ignored it.

'This pre-nuptial agreement may well become public and the Prince must be seen as doing the right thing by you and his son,' she'd been told, and once again she'd subsided.

As she'd subsided in everything. At least Michales would always be well provided for.

But now... The organ blared into its triumphant wedding march. Reality was suddenly right here. She'd been pushed off the end of the royal conveyor belt and here she was, about to be married.

She wasn't...her. She was inside some creature wearing full bridal gear, extravagant to the point of ridiculous, inside a cathedral, about to be married.

It wasn't Lily who was doing this. It was someone else. Lily was trapped inside.

The doors swung open. At the end of the aisle... Alex.

For two weeks she'd blocked him almost completely from her mind. She was about to be married but this wasn't about Alex. It wasn't about either of them.

Maybe her decision to walk down the aisle on her own had been a mistake. She wouldn't mind Spiros's arm to lean on right now. She wouldn't mind anything to lean on.

She needed to start walking.

Alex was waiting.

No. She told herself that sharply. It wasn't Alex. Just as she was trapped inside someone else, the man at the end of the aisle was a stranger, some prince in his regimentals, waiting to marry a woman in a gown of shimmering beaded lace, with a glorious train trailing twenty feet behind her, with a three-tiered veil attached with a tiara, which had come straight from the royal vaults, the dresser had breathed. Worth a king's ransom.

Her legs felt frozen.

Do this and get it over with, she told herself.

Everyone was looking at her. Everyone was waiting.

Deep breath. Do this and get on with your life.

She looked along the aisle and Alex was smiling at her.

Her prince.

No. If she thought *Prince* her feet wouldn't move.

She had to get a grip on what was reality and what wasn't. This was Alex smiling at her. The father of her child.

This wedding was a fantasy, but the fantasy had a name.

Alex.

She stepped forward and she looked directly at her waiting bridegroom. She forced herself to smile back.

She could do this.

She could be married to Alex.

He'd suggested she have Spiros give her away. But…

'No,' she'd told him. 'Eleni's taking care of Michales during the ceremony. That's all I'll ask of them. If I ever get married for real I want Spiros to give me away then. But not now. Not for a marriage of convenience.'

So she was alone. He hadn't realised quite how alone until he saw the cathedral doors swing open. She was standing quite still, quite calm. She looked as determined on this course as she'd been from the moment she'd agreed to his proposal.

'You know, this could work,' Nikos said from beside him.

Alex was watching Lily walk steadily towards him, regal and lovely, her head held high, the magnificent gown making her look almost ethereal. He was forcing himself to smile at her as the congregation were clearly expecting him to do—but something inside him was twisting. Hurting.

'Why the hell wouldn't it work?' he growled.

'The islanders hated the idea of another Mia,' Nikos whispered. 'But you just need to look at Lily to see she's not like her sister. Mia had twelve bridesmaids. Mia had so much bling you couldn't see her for glitter. Lily's different. Simple and lovely.'

Simple and lovely… They weren't words Alex would have thought appropriate for a royal bride.

But they were right.

Lily was not doing this for money. His cheque remained in its pieces—or maybe it had been burned long since—and it had never been replaced. She'd even tried to refuse the allowance his lawyers had written into the pre-nuptial contracts should they ever divorce. 'You can pay for Michales's upbringing and nothing else,' she'd said.

This wedding…this marriage…it seemed she was doing this for Sappheiros. She wanted nothing from it.

He didn't believe it yet. He couldn't. The anger and disbelief he'd held ever since he'd learned of Michales's true parentage still simmered.

Do this and get it over with.

She'd almost reached him. He smiled and she smiled back, but he knew her smile was as forced as his.

This wasn't the smile he knew from a year ago. This wasn't the Lily he'd made love to. This was a stranger, a woman coerced.

He had an almost irresistible impulse to take her hand and walk out, right there and then. Before this mock marriage could take place. Not because he didn't want it. But because…it felt intrinsically wrong.

She'd agreed to this marriage for all the wrong reasons.

He took her hand and it was icy. Unresponsive.

She looked trapped.

She'd trapped herself by bearing his child, he thought grimly. By agreeing to Mia and Giorgos's great lie.

Forget it, he told himself harshly. Forget the lie. Concentrate on now. Concentrate on the need to be married.

So be it.

Her smile had faded as she'd realised he'd only been smiling for the sake of their audience. He watched a fleeting shadow of something…hurt?…pass over her face.

Why should she be hurt?

This was a formal ceremony and they had to get on.

'Why not ask Father Antonio to marry you?' Nikos had asked, and he hadn't answered. But he knew the answer.

When—if!—he married for real he'd be married by Father Antonio.

This was a royal marriage of convenience. Nothing more.

Lily's hand stayed in his. They faced the Archbishop together.

'We are gathered together to join this man and this woman…'

The formal reception was attended by every person of significance from the Diamond Isles and beyond. In the vast marquee erected in the palace grounds, on the headland overlooking Sappheiros Bay, there were speeches, speeches and more speeches.

This wasn't the simple celebration of a wedding. This was the celebration of three nations finding independence and hope. The islanders' joy had little to do with Lily and Alex.

Lily may have provided this outcome but the consensus among the crowd, the media and by the islanders in general, was that she'd done very well for herself. Where was the need for sympathy?

Or even…civility?

As the day wore on Alex was congratulated by islander after islander, but the eyes that watched his bride were guarded.

She was Mia's sister, and Mia was hated. Like Mia, Lily was suspected as being a woman who'd conned her way into being a part of the royal dynasty.

Alex could do little to protect her. The slurs weren't overt. They were subtle looks, subtle congratulations with the islanders looking only at him, refusing to meet Lily's gaze as hands were shaken.

But, he had to admit, despite the slurs, despite the guarded looks, she was behaving…beautifully. She was a lovely bride—serene and almost breathtakingly lovely. But she was so quiet. He'd pulled her veil back from her face for the obligatory kiss-the-bride, but she hadn't responded as he'd done so and he had the feeling that her veil was down again, metaphorically if not literally.

She hardly spoke through the formal luncheon and the formal reception. She responded civilly to those who spoke to her but her responses were muted.

He'd catch her glance straying over and over to Eleni, who was holding Michales.

She wanted her baby back and her look said she wanted more. She wanted her life back?

The civilities had to be borne—he could no sooner escape than she could. But as the afternoon stretched towards evening he decided *enough*. A band had started playing and a dance floor was laid across the lawns. The festivities would continue into the small hours. But...

'You want to escape?' he asked and saw a flare of hope, unable to be disguised.

'Can we?'

'This party will go on without us. I have a place on the other side of the island.' He'd thought of this yesterday when Nikos had asked about honeymoon plans. They had to be seen as doing something—but this was no time to be away from the island.

He hadn't wanted to take Lily to his own home but unless they stayed in the palace here there was little choice. And the thought of staying in the palace—obligatory appearance on the balcony—prince kisses bride—left him cold.

'A place?' she asked.

'A house. We can be private there.'

'What, for a honeymoon?' It was said wryly. She'd schooled herself to do this, he thought. Maybe if he insisted on his conjugal rights she'd submit as well. To outward appearance she looked beautiful and serene and untroubled. Maybe even submissive?

Maybe submissive was the wrong word. It was definitely

the wrong word if this was the Lily he'd met little more than a year ago.

But how well did he know her? Not well, but enough to guess that behind the serenity was quiet desperation.

'We're expected to go away for a bit. I can't go far, but I have a house on the north end of the island.'

'So…you and me and how many servants?'

'Just you and me.' Then, as he saw another fear flare, 'And Michales,' he added swiftly.

Her relief was immediate and obvious. 'I can take him?'

'Of course.'

She closed her eyes and he thought she was trying desperately to disguise what she was thinking. How fearfully out of control she felt?

It didn't make sense. Was she afraid of him? Afraid of the royalty bit? Surely not. She *was* Mia's sister.

'We can go now?' she asked.

'Yes.'

'Then what are we waiting for?'

CHAPTER SEVEN

THEY were to depart in a bridal coach. A gold-painted barouche with the Sappheiros coat of arms emblazoned on the panels, with white leather upholstery and white satin cushions—something straight out of *Cinderella*.

It took only this, Lily thought in disbelief. Alex handed her up into the coach. Attendants arranged her skirts and her train, tucking her in with care.

Alex climbed up and sat beside her.

Eleni handed up Michales.

This had been a crazy day. She was about as far from her comfort zone as she'd ever want to be. But this…this was just plain fantasy. This was every girl's dream—being whisked off in a golden coach with Prince Charming.

In the fairy tales she'd read, babies weren't included. But Michales definitely was.

So… Her Prince Charming was sitting beside her. He looked absurdly handsome—regal and tasselled and armed with sword and all the things a Prince Of The Blood should be.

She probably even looked like a princess, she conceded. All white satin and lace and exquisite beading—and there were diamonds in her tiara, for heaven's sake.

There were four white horses in their traces, heads held high, shiny, sleek, gold harnesses, bits and assorted leather stuff. They had gold and white attachments and white-feathered headdresses—did horses wear headdresses? These ones did, she decided. They looked fabulous.

Even the coachman looked amazing. His uniform was almost as ornate as Alex's—only he was wearing a top hat.

There were sixteen more horsemen, eight in front and eight behind. Horseguards?

Was one of them carrying a diaper bag? She daren't ask. She hoped someone had thought of it, but the royal princess standing up and asking for diapers…maybe not.

The desire to giggle grew even stronger.

Michales jiggled on her knee. She hugged him. He crowed with delight and squirmed and tried to reach her tiara.

It was too much. She burst out laughing and Alex stared at her as if she'd entirely lost it.

'What the…?'

'Cinderella and Prince Charming—and Baby,' she told him, and grinned and lifted the unprotesting Michales across to his father's knee. 'Here. You hold him. He's not very good with travelling.'

'What do you mean?'

'I suspect you might find out for yourself,' she said and chuckled again at the expression on his face. Then, as it seemed to be expected of her—she'd seen the odd royal wedding on the telly—she turned and smiled broadly at the crowd. She waved!

If he could be a prince, she could be a princess.

'I might find out what for myself?' he said cautiously.

'You'll know it when it happens,' she said sagely. 'Aren't you supposed to be waving?'

'I appear to be needing to hang on.'

'That's all right,' she said magnanimously. 'You hold on and I'll wave for the two of us.'

This was dumb but she couldn't stop grinning. She was so far out of her comfort zone that she ought to be a quivering wreck. But she'd just got through a royal wedding and she hadn't fallen over once. As far as she knew, she hadn't said anything stupid.

She was married.

This was no real marriage, she told herself. She surely intended staying…well, not married in the true sense of the word. But she was married and she wasn't afraid of Alex. She didn't trust him, but then maybe she didn't have to trust. This was a business arrangement. If she could just keep her cool, keep her independence, maybe she could even enjoy this—just a bit.

Maybe that was hysteria speaking.

Just wave to the crowds, pin your smile in place and try not to think of the man sitting beside you with your baby on his lap, she told herself.

Her baby's father.

Her…husband.

This was crazy. He didn't belong here.

Hell, he had to do this. The islanders needed him to be Crown Prince but every nerve in his body was screaming at him to get out of here, get back to Manhattan, go into his office, slam the door on the outside world and design a garden or six.

For the last ten years garden design had been his life. As a child, his only friends had been the palace servants. An old gardener had taken him under his wing, and the palace garden had become an enormous pleasure.

When his mother had been permitted to return to the island they'd designed a garden, and the two years they had together had seen it become a wondrous living thing.

Then, when he'd joined the army to finally get away from his uncle, to achieve financial independence, he'd kept on designing. He'd sent in an entry to an international competition.

That entry had changed his life.

This wasn't his life, he told himself savagely. It was the last lingering trace of Giorgos's reign. Lily was sister to the last Queen. This woman sitting beside him, waving to the crowd, her smile wide and genuine, was a fairy tale princess. Like Mia, she was playing a part. In time she could move on.

Whereas he…he was stuck with reality.

In the shape of his son?

It wasn't just that, though the sensation of a small robust person sitting on his knee was certainly unnerving. It was the whole set-up.

As an idealistic youngster he'd dreamed of ruling this country, of being able to do what he had to do to make the island prosper. He'd dreamed of being given the authority to do it.

He'd never dreamed of this. He was in a fairy tale coach with a fairy tale wife and a tiny son.

She was looking as if she enjoyed it.

Maybe she was better at pretending than he was.

This was so…fake. The only problem was, though, that when he woke in the morning it would be worse. There were so many problems. He'd take a couple of days out of the frame here to get this marriage thing settled and over, but he had to get back. Two or three days' honeymoon…

It wasn't really a honeymoon.

Lily was waving at the crowd as if she meant it. She was enjoying herself?

Maybe he could use this to his advantage, he thought suddenly. If she was to be accepted by the islanders…she could stay here and play princess. He could still make the important decisions but it might give him time to escape to his other life. The garden designs he loved.

It was worth a thought. Lily as a figurehead.

Maybe…maybe…

Maybe this was too soon to tell. There was no way he was going to trust her.

She was doing okay now. Better than he was.

She was better at pretending. Better at…deceiving?

He looked out over the crowd of onlookers. There were those in the crowd who wished him ill. There were those who wanted this fledgling principality to fail so they could gather the remains.

He had to do this. He had no choice.

His bride was by his side and she was waving. It seemed he was part of a royal family, even if that family was as fractured as his family always had been.

He waved.

'My smile hurts,' Lily whispered.

'My face aches,' he confessed.

'Really?' She swivelled to stare. 'But you're used to this.'

'I'm a landscape architect. Not a prince.' He shook his head. 'No. This is what I wanted. It just feels too ridiculous for words.'

'Just smile and wave,' she said wisely. 'It doesn't matter if no one's at home.'

'If no one's at home…'

'Anyone can be royal. Plan your gardens in your head while you wave.' She waved a bit more and smiled a bit more. 'Look at me. I'm getting good at it.'

'So you…'

'I'm planning boats.'

They'd swung out of the palace grounds now. People were coming out of their houses to see them go past.

They had eight outriders behind and eight in front.

Lily waved to an elderly couple standing in their garden. The old man didn't wave back but the old woman almost did. She lifted her hand—and then thought better of it.

'They still think I'm like Mia,' Lily said, stoically waving. 'Just lucky I'm not taking this personally.'

'Yeah,' he said. He waved and the old man and woman immediately waved back.

'You must have sex appeal,' Lily said sagely. 'Or something.'

'They know me.'

'They're never going to know me,' Lily said and it sounded as if the idea was comforting.

He should be reassured by that. But there was a stab of jealousy. And something more…

The only places Lily had seen on Sappheiros had been the royal palace and the chapel-cum-cathedral in its grounds. They'd been enough to take her breath away—all spires and turrets and opulence in a fairy tale setting, the sapphire coast-line backed by mountains. The palace and cathedral were way over-the-top for a small country, she'd thought, but still, royal was royal, and she'd assumed the whole of the Diamond Isles must be in favour of a bit of pomp and splendour.

Now she wasn't so sure. The coastal road was lined with houses that looked shabby, some almost derelict. From what she'd learned over the last two weeks, the people had been taxed to the hilt to pay for the kings' follies.

Now Alex told her he was taking her to his private house. He'd been raised as nephew to the King. For much of his life he'd been first in line to the throne, so she assumed his home would be opulent as well.

Their retinue slowed as they came to a curve in a road that had been getting rougher the further they'd travelled from the city. At one time it must have been paved, but the bitumen was cracked now and giving way. The coastal road—a magnificent route set halfway up the cliffs and overlooking the sea—swept around a headland and on, but the coach slowed by a sign that said—discreetly—'Hideaway'.

The coach stopped, as did the outriders.

Alex stepped down onto the track and held out a hand to help her down.

'Um…where are we?' She gazed around her with surprise. They were in the middle of nowhere. A beautiful nowhere but nowhere nevertheless.

'We need to walk,' he said.

'Walk.'

'It's a rhododendron drive. It's too low for the horses to go underneath.'

'These guys can't take off their fancy headgear?' She gazed round at the impassive horsemen. The horses were standing motionless. There was not a blink from man or horse.

'From this gate we're not royal,' he said, so softly only she could hear. 'This road has been deliberately left so the royal vehicles can't get through.'

'Right.' But it wasn't right. She didn't understand. This was where the fairy tale stopped?

They needed to walk? Fine if you were wearing glossy black boots and a sword to slash the undergrowth. She had four-inch heels and a twenty-foot train.

But she was almost past worrying. Hysteria was carrying her along nicely—as well as her innate sense of the ridiculous.

'Okay then,' she said, and she thought she even sounded hysterical. 'We walk. Did you bring scroggin?'

'Scroggin?' he said blankly.

'Food for serious hikers. You can't go more than twenty miles without it.'

He grinned. 'What about three hundred yards? Or I could bring the Jeep down to fetch you. Sorry about this, but this place is private. We don't want horseguards on our honeymoon.'

'No,' she said cautiously.

Honeymoon.

Right.

Alex had obviously been planning this. Yeah, she could see that about him. A planner.

It made her nervous. Or more nervous. How nervous could she get?

Concentrate on practicalities, she told herself. Here she was, in full bridal attire, stuck in the middle of nowhere.

With a baby. Once again the issue of a diaper bag raised its head.

'There is the small matter of our baggage,' she said cautiously. 'Much as I love being a bride, this look could get a bit over-the-top at breakfast. And you get to look after Michales if there are no clean diapers.'

'Our luggage was brought here earlier.'

She gulped. And nodded. 'Of course it was. So we were always coming here?'

'Did you want to stay in the palace?'

'It all depends,' she said and picked up her skirts. 'On what I find at the end of this rhododendron drive. Thanks, guys,' she said to their escort and waved but they didn't respond by one fraction of a lift of an eyebrow.

She wasn't much good at this princess business.

Just lucky it was temporary.

She looked sideways at her temporary husband.

'Okay,' she said. 'If you didn't bring the scroggin, then we'd better move fast.' She faced up the track and took a deep breath and started walking. She was aware that Alex watched her for a minute without moving. Why? Surely the sight of a bride trudging into a gloom of rhododendrons must be commonplace!

But finally he followed, carrying her son.

She turned and looked—and then looked away again fast. The sight of Alex with Michales had the power to make her feel…hungry?

Hungry for what? She wasn't sure.

'You're good,' he said as he caught up with her. They were out of sight—and out of earshot of their outriders now.

'At hiking? I'd like to see you hike in heels this high.'

'I couldn't,' he admitted. 'But that's not what I was saying. You were great today.'

'I did what I had to do,' she said, stalking on as purposefully as four-inch heels allowed. 'The islanders don't like me, but that's okay. I won't be staying here long enough for it to matter.'

'A year,' he said.

'That's what the deal is.'

'Unless we want more.'

She stopped. Uh-oh. There were things to clear up here before they went an inch further.

'Alex, let's get this straight,' she said, making her voice firm. Or as firm as it was possible to get when her breathing wouldn't work properly. 'There are two things I want in life and only two.'

'And they would be?'

You, she thought, but there was no way she was telling Alex that. She was afraid of even admitting it to herself.

'My son and my boats,' she managed. 'I might be able to squash a marriage of convenience in at the edges but that's all. If anything—*anything*—gets in the way of my two priorities then I'm out of here.'

'You don't want to be a fairy tale princess?'

'That's Mia's department. I'm just me.'

'It's possible to compromise,' he said softly. 'That's why I brought you here.'

'To teach me to compromise. No deal. I told you…'

'Your baby and your boats. Yes, you did. I get that loud and clear. But there's also the fact that we have a country to govern.'

'You, kiddo,' she snapped.

'I need your help.'

'For what? I've done the fairy tale bit. This train is so heavy…'

'I need you to help me create stability,' he said. He took her train from her grasp so he was holding her son and the sheer weight of her gown. He met her look so steadily that she thought for a blind, dumb moment that he was sex on legs and she was married to him for real. She fought a fast internal fight and managed a sensible reply.

'How can I do that when the islanders hate me?'

'They don't hate you. They don't know you.'

'Which is fine.'

'Which would have been fine if I hadn't seduced you…'

She gasped. 'What the…?' Whoa. Where was he going with this?

There was no way she was continuing this hike into nowhere if he stayed believing that. 'If I remember rightly, it was me who seduced you,' she snapped. 'Did I not?'

He looked a bit…stunned. 'I can't remember,' he admitted.

'You said that before. Any minute now you'll tell me you were drunk.'

'I wasn't drunk. I remember every part of that last night.'

'Me, too,' she said. 'It was a truly excellent night. But it wasn't me playing the pathetic part of Sleeping Beauty, leaving the action solely to my prince. I'm your equal in every way and I have rights. We made love once and we were stupid. We were both stupid. So get over it.' She grabbed her train, turned and walked on a few steps, then swore, removed her shoes and picked up the pace.

He let her go. She was holding her own train again. She looked…free, he thought and was hit by a stab of pure, unadulterated jealousy. And more…

His bride, running under the dark canopy, looking nothing at all like Mia, nothing at all like any woman he'd ever met.

She was still wearing her veil and her headpiece. She was still a bride. If he wasn't holding Michales…

She emerged from the tunnel of rhododendrons, angry and confused.

She saw Alex's house and she forgot angry and confused. She forgot everything.

It was as if a wand had been waved, transforming the world from a dark, threatening place into sheer fantasy. Not fantasy as in the over-the-top royal palace. Fantasy as in sheer delight.

The house had been built into the cliffs. It was a white-washed villa, built on three levels, with winding steps joining each level. There were rocky ledges between each level, with bench seats and tables so someone could conceivably carry a drink down towards the beach and pause at each bend, to sit and admire the view.

There were flowers everywhere, spilling from every crevice, so the rock face was bursting with colour. Bougainvillea—crimson, pinks and deep, deep burgundy. There were daisies, growing as if birds had dropped their seeds and they'd simply grown where they'd been dropped. A great twisted vine of wisteria seemed to hold the place together, its gnarled, knotted wood adorned with vast sprays of soft, glorious blues.

The house looked deceptively simple, built of stone, weathered to beauty, appearing to be almost part of the cliffs. Tiny balconies protruded from each window, joining the intricate flow of steps down to the beach.

And, below the house, the sea—sapphire, translucent, magic. A tiny cove. A wooden dinghy hauled up on the sand.

There were even a couple of dolphins in the bay.

Lily stopped and stared. It was all she could do not to cry out in delight.

'The dolphins…'

'I pay 'em to do that,' Alex said, coming up behind her. He smiled. 'Welcome home.'

'I… It's not my home,' she whispered, awed.

'You've married me. I guess in a sense it is your home.'

'Does the pre-nup say I get half?' she said before she could stop herself, and kept right on gazing, eager to convince herself that this was real, that this wasn't some *Cinderella* fairy tale. There was no midnight looming here, for fantasy to return this place to mice and pumpkins.

Or maybe there was but she couldn't think of that right now. This place was seductive in its loveliness.

She could play with Michales on this beach. Maybe she could stay here for the year of their marriage. There'd be no need to juggle work and baby care. The terror in her head was gone.

Here she could be free.

Her eyes filled with tears. She brushed them away fiercely, angrily, but still they came.

Alex was beside her, calmly handing her a handkerchief.

She took it and blew her nose. Defiant.

'What's wrong?' he asked, but he was still smiling and she had to suspect he knew exactly what was wrong.

'This would have to be the most seductive setting in the known universe,' she whispered.

'You're the first woman I've ever brought here.'

She sniffed. She looked at him with suspicion over the top of his handkerchief. 'And that has to be the most seductive line,' she managed, trying to sound caustic—and failing.

'You don't trust me?'

'Would you trust you?' She waved his handkerchief at the scene in front of her. 'Would you trust yourself?'

'It's great, isn't it?'

'You built this garden?' She hesitated. 'Of course you built it. You're a landscape architect. I read about it. You've won prizes.'

'You build boats. I design gardens.'

'Here?'

'Not many,' he admitted. 'I mostly work out of Manhattan.'

That was confusing. 'Are you still working in Manhattan?'

'When I can. As often as I can get away from here.'

Whoa. Panic! 'You mean you're going back to Manhattan?'

'You don't want me here, do you?' He shrugged. 'I'd assumed you'd stay in the palace, play with Spiros and your boats and your son. I need to put some solid work into rebuilding this economy but if I can manage to get that sorted then I'm free to do what I want.'

Where was the problem with that? She stared down at the cove. Thinking. Or trying to think.

There were factors at play here she hadn't thought of. She felt as if she were floating in a bubble—she was precariously safe within, but any minute it could burst. What was outside? Who knew?

'Do you swim?' he asked.

'Of course.' In the midst of confusion, here was something solid.

'I feel a swim coming on,' he said, and why did she feel he was changing the subject? 'We have an hour or so before dusk. Can you bear to take off your wedding dress?'

'I can't wait to take off my wedding dress.' Then, dumbly, she felt herself blushing. 'I mean…'

'I know what you mean,' he told her. 'You'll have a separate apartment here, too.'

Great. It was great. Wasn't it?

'But Michales…' she managed.

'He's almost six months old. Shouldn't he be surfing by now?'

'How long can we stay here?' she asked, staring longingly down at the cove. The dolphins had been joined by friends. They were catching waves, surfing in amazing synchronisation, then performing sleek tumbling turns and gliding out to catch more.

It looked fantastic. How could she think of anything but the sight before her?

'You can stay for two weeks maybe,' he told her. 'I need to go earlier.'

Suddenly she didn't want to know. She didn't want to think past this moment.

'Then we're wasting time. Those dolphins are in my waves. Let's swim.'

CHAPTER EIGHT

HE NEEDED to swim. He needed to get rid of some pent-up energy.

He needed to clear his head.

Half an hour later they were all in the water. Lily was sitting in the shallows, letting Michales kick his delight as tiny waves broke over his toes. Leaving him free.

Which was what he wanted. Wasn't it?

Of course it was.

He was doing backstroke, back and forth across the cove so he could watch her as he swam. He needed to let her be. But he could watch her in the shallows, holding Michales, watching him splash, absorbed in her son.

He didn't have a handle on her. He'd met her once and been entranced. She'd said she'd seduced him, and to a certain extent it was true. Her laughter had seduced him, her loveliness, her vibrancy. Today, standing in the rhododendron drive in full bridal finery, discussing scroggin, he'd seen that part of her again. It was as if it had somehow resurfaced, despite herself.

Resurfaced… That was the problem. His gut was telling him this was the real Lily. Only she'd handed her baby—*his* baby— to her sister. She'd made one phone call to him and then abandoned the idea of telling him.

It didn't fit. The Lily he thought he knew would have appeared on his doorstep, angry as hell, tossing her pregnancy to him as she'd tossed the idea of seduction. It was something they'd shared. It was something they'd taken responsibility for together.

There were two Lilys. The Lily he knew—and either a conniving Lily or some other Lily. He couldn't cope with the idea of either.

Whichever was right, they had to achieve some way of facing the world together. But first…how were they going to get through these first few days?

By avoidance? They'd changed in their separate apartments, and they'd met on the steps coming down to the beach.

She was wearing a plain black bathing costume and another of her lovely scarves.

She'd made him feel…confused as hell.

Dammit, a woman was not going to mess with his head. He couldn't afford confusion. He had to put every bit of energy he possessed into getting this island back on its feet. He needed to get it back to where it just needed a figurehead.

Could Lily be part of that figurehead?

She'd reacted with fear.

He didn't understand what was going on. He didn't understand her.

He swam and swam.

This was the only way to go, he told himself. Get yourself so physically tired you can forget her.

Right.

This place was fabulous. She sat in the shallows with her baby son and the frisson of excitement she'd had when she'd first arrived resurfaced.

Freedom had many guises. Staying here, with Michales, could be a form of freedom. Only Alex's initial statement that this was her home had been quickly rescinded. Two weeks… Then the palace.

There were issues here she hadn't thought about. Alex's

work, for one. If he thought she was staying in the palace while he swanned off back to Manhattan…

No deal.

He was swimming back and forth. Back and forth. It was as if he was driven.

He hated royalty. She'd figured that.

Did he plan one day to escape and leave Michales and her to represent royalty in their own rights? When the islanders hated her? Not likely.

But she couldn't trust him.

She closed her eyes. Michales was kicking his feet in delight, splashing them both. Suddenly she was hit by an almost overwhelming longing. For someone to trust.

Her father had been in his sixties when she was born. She'd been his carer. He'd depended on her but she'd always known that when her father looked at her, he only saw echoes of the young, fascinating wife who'd deserted him. He always saw pain. Her mother and Mia had abandoned her. Mia had betrayed her in the worst possible way.

You didn't do trust. Not ever.

But she gazed out at Alex and she couldn't stop the feeling of indescribable pain washing through. He was her husband but she was still alone.

Not alone. Michales depended on her.

She needed to be practical and firm—for Michales's sake.

She needed to remember who she was. A mother, yes. And a boat-builder.

Not a lover. Not a wife.

A boat-builder.

She turned deliberately from watching Alex and looked instead up the beach.

She'd been absorbed in the antics of her small son. But suddenly he saw her attention turn to the old dinghy high on the sand. She rose, cradled Michales against her and strolled up the beach to inspect the boat.

Michales waved his hands indignantly towards the sea, where the dolphins were still cavorting far out. Alex sensed her smile from this distance. She walked back to the shallows and started playing again.

She should have time to look at the boat if she wanted.

He didn't want to go near either of them. The same feeling he'd had in the coach came flooding back. Family, he reminded himself.

He did not do family.

Maybe he could go back to the castle. There was pressure mounting from all sides. If he went quietly back, maybe the press wouldn't discover he'd abandoned Lily here.

Maybe if he left she might feel safer, he thought. He could leave her here to have a holiday in the sun with her baby.

Meanwhile, he could get himself organised. Get this damned island organised. Meet with Nikos and Stefanos and see what they could figure out.

Leave Lily?

Yeah, that felt good. Not.

They were his family.

He didn't do family.

Love meant grief and loss and heartache.

She wanted to look at the boat. Okay, he could take Michales for a bit. That small commitment wouldn't hurt.

He swam slowly in to shore, catching a wave for the last part, letting the surf sweep him on. He ended up right beside her. Too close.

She rose, stepping away from him, making space.

'Sorry.' He swiped the water from his eyes, kneeling in the shallows. 'I should have been taking turns with Michales.'

'It's your turn now,' she said and suddenly he had his arms full of baby. And, astonishingly, her voice had turned indignant.

'Did you know you have a treasure of a boat up there? She's a gorgeous old clinker-built dinghy, planked in King Billy Pine with Huon Pine and a Kauri transom. What the hell are you doing, letting her rot?'

'I… She's old,' he said, astounded by her sudden passion. 'My father brought her here before I was born. I took her out a couple of years ago and knocked a hole in her on the rocks.'

'So she's been sitting on the beach since then.' Indignant wasn't the half of it. She made it sound as if he'd murdered a puppy.

'She's got a hole in her.'

'You'd have a hole in you, too, if you'd hit a rock. That's a reason for abandoning her?' She was stalking up the beach towards the wreck, letting him follow if he wanted.

He followed, carrying Michales. She had a really cute butt.

Um…think of something else, he told himself. He'd put a hole in the boat. He was the bad guy?

Michales yelled. Lurched his small body back towards the water. Yelled some more.

'He wants more swimming,' Lily said without looking back. He wants…

He definitely wanted. Michales's full focus was on the waves.

Alex's father had taught him to swim. It was the only memory he had of his father—blurred by time but with him still. He was floating in the water, his father's big hands under his tummy, coaxing him to push off, to see if he could float if his father's hands weren't there.

And when he had…his father whirling him round and round, spinning with excitement, calling out to his mother, *'He's done it—our son can swim.'*

Now it was…his turn?

He walked slowly back into the water, to just beyond the breaking waves. He dipped his son into the sea. He held him under his tummy.

Michales was far too young to coax as his father had coaxed

him. But Michales figured out the basics as if he'd been born to the waves.

Balanced on his father's hands, his legs and arms went like little windmills. He was a ball of splashing, chortling delight. He had no fear. He knew his father's hands would keep him safe.

His son.

Lily was up the beach, inspecting his old boat.

His wife.

The sensations were almost overwhelming.

But then his thoughts were interrupted. Out to sea, a boat rounded the headland. A cruiser. Thirty feet long or more. New.

There were a couple of men in the bow and they had binoculars in their hands. Or cameras.

Hell, he'd wanted privacy. He might have known reporters would try and get in here.

He lifted Michales into his arms. The little boy must have finally had enough. He snuggled into his father's bare chest— and here were more of those sensations he didn't know what to do with.

He strode up the beach to his wife. *His wife.* She was still focused on the boat.

'Lily, let's go,' he said urgently.

'Why?'

'These people…' He motioned back towards the cruiser and she glanced at it without interest. 'I suspect they're reporters.'

'So?' To his frustration, her attention was all on the boat. She'd crouched down to look closer. 'She's looking great for two years stuck on the beach. Look at the workmanship. All she needs is a couple of new spars and calking. New expoxy resin. I could make her fabulous.' The edge of one side of the boat was half buried in the sand and she started digging.

'Lily…'

'I want to see if this is intact. I bet it is. I'm wondering if the sand's been covering her. Sometimes boats buried in the sand can last for half a century or so before they start rotting, especially if the sand stays dry.'

'I don't want these people to photograph you.'

'Why not?'

Good question, he thought. Because she wasn't glamorous? Because she wasn't made-up for the cameras?

She was wearing a cheap, ill-fitting bathing costume and no make-up. Her short-cropped curls clung wetly around her face, escaping from her wetly limp scarf. Did she care?

'Look at the rear thwart,' she said reverently. 'It's gorgeous. That's Huon pine. Tasmania's the only place it grows. It's a dream of mine, to build a boat all of Huon, only of course there's so little left. Those babies take centuries to grow. The Tasmanians flooded a valley last century and they're diving for the timber now. If I could get some…'

She was lost, he thought, fascinated. She had eyes only for the boat.

The cruiser had come into shallow waters. Two men jumped overboard.

With cameras.

They were photographing as they came, as if expecting any minute they'd be noticed and their quarry would run.

Lily wouldn't run, he thought. Not the first Lily he'd met. Not the passionate Lily. Not when she had her hands on a sick boat.

Real Huon pine. Her eyes were shining with missionary zeal.

'Lily…'

She didn't look up. He groaned inwardly but gave up. How could you protect someone from herself?

Did she want protecting?

His protectiveness was mixing with something else now. Pride?

The thought was novel but there it was. She knew the reporters were here, but she wasn't losing concentration. She'd finished digging out the side of the boat and was running her fingers gently round the timbers. Taking in every square inch of the ancient dinghy.

'Can I fix it for you?' she asked.

'It's a wreck.'

'It's not a wreck. Look at these timbers. They look almost as watertight as the day she was made. All she needs is lots of TLC.'

'TLC?'

'Tender loving care,' she said and ran her hands over the old timbers with such a look on her face that he felt…

Jealous?

Whoa, that was nuts.

He was holding Michales. Michales was gazing down at his mother as well.

'You've been usurped,' he told the baby ruefully. 'Your mother's fallen in love with a boat.' But then he figured maybe he'd better pay attention to the press. The two men were getting closer. Their trousers were wet from wading ashore. They were snapping for all they were worth, as if they thought they were about to be thrown off the beach.

He should have brought a couple of security guys down here. Instinctively, he moved to put his body between Lily and the photographers but, apart from one uninterested glance, all Lily's focus was on the boat.

'Ma'am?' the younger man called and Lily tore her attention from the boat again.

'Lily,' she corrected him. 'I don't do ma'am.' She'd spoken in Greek, almost absently. Now she went back to inspecting the boat.

The photographers were taken aback. Whatever they'd expected of her, it wasn't this.

He'd allowed no press conferences before the wedding. There'd been such hostility towards her that he'd worried she'd get a really hard time—certainly be treated with contempt. Now he thought maybe a restricted conference might have been better—with pre-approved questions. As it was, these men knew nothing about her and they were able to ask anything.

The first question was harmless enough. 'You speak Greek?'

'Yes.'

'Queen Mia didn't.'

She sighed as if vaguely irritated but not much. 'Mia and I were raised by different parents. My father taught me Greek. My maternal relatives were Greek and they taught me boatbuilding. My boss is Greek and I like learning. Okay?'

'Are you really Mia's sister?'

She didn't answer straight away. Instead, she crawled around to the other side of the boat where the hole was a gaping mass of shattered timber. She touched the fragments of timber as a doctor might touch a fractured arm—with all the care in the world.

'Of course I am,' she said at last, without looking up.

'And the baby… He's really yours?'

'Michales really is mine,' she agreed. 'Prince Alexandros has proved it. Who wants to know?'

'Just about all the world.'

'So how did you feel when you discovered the Queen had stolen your baby?' one of the reporters asked and Alex stopped thinking about language. How could she answer this?

But she didn't even have to think about it. 'There's no need to be melodramatic.' She was using her hands to measure the width of the hole. 'Mia didn't steal him. I was ill and she cared for him.'

'And passed him off as her own.'

'I know nothing about that,' she said. 'Mia cared for my little boy, and when I was well enough I came here to fetch him. Alex supports me. So what else do you want to know?'

She'd said it as if what had happened was an everyday occurrence. As if there was no controversy at all.

'Prince Alex says he didn't know he was your baby's father.'

The younger man had lowered his camera and was holding out a voice recorder. Alex thought about objecting, but then thought *why*? Maybe Lily's calm pragmatism was just what was called for.

What the country needed?

What he needed.

She didn't seem to be aware that she looked…dowdy.

No, he thought. Dowdy was the wrong word. A woman as cute as Lily could never look dowdy. Her swimsuit must have been bought before her illness—it was too big for her. Her nose was turning pink from the sun. Her scarf was slipping backwards, and her curls were twisting in damp tendrils across her forehead.

Cute? More. She was gorgeous. He was starting to feel…

'Yes, I was dumb enough not to tell him,' she said to the reporters. She might have been discussing the weather.

'Why didn't you?'

'I had my reasons.' She sounded a bit irritated. But then she seemed to think about it. She sat back on her heels and gazed up at Alex, as if assessing him and rethinking her answer.

'You know, the first time I met Prince Alex I thought he was wonderful,' she admitted. 'But I was ill and on medication and maybe I wasn't myself. Alex didn't know I was ill—or pregnant—only a rat would have taken advantage of me and you must know by now that the Prince is an honourable man. Now that Alex knows the truth, he's made me an honest woman. I intend to stay here with my son and my husband, build boats and live happily ever after. I'll start with repairing this one. Is that okay with you?'

What were the reporters supposed to say to that? They were staring at her, open-mouthed. It was so obviously not a rehearsed speech that she'd taken their breath away.

She'd taken his breath away.

She'd been ill.

She'd downplayed it, but suddenly he thought, *how ill*?

She'd said it before, but it had been brushed aside. She'd implied she'd had a minor operation. Maybe she'd had morning sickness as well.

But…ill when she'd conceived?

And…she'd made their marriage sound ordinary.

He wouldn't have minded if she'd looked up and smiled at him, formed some sort of connection to make these guys think that their initial attraction still held.

To make *him* think that initial attraction still held.

Hell, what was he thinking? One part of him wanted a marriage of convenience. The rest of him wanted to claim this woman as his.

Which was ridiculous. What had changed to make him trust her?

'Do you have any more questions?' she asked, rising and wiping sand from her hands on the sides of her bathing suit. 'Michales has been in the sun for long enough. I need to take him up to the house.' She lifted Michales from Alex's grasp and waited—politely—for the reporters to leave.

'Are you in love with Prince Alex?' the older reporter asked and Alex drew in his breath. Of all the impertinences…

But Lily didn't seem perturbed.

'I'd imagine half the hot-blooded women in the western world are in love with His Highness,' she said and she grinned. 'Ask your readers.'

'But your marriage…'

'The Prince is an honourable man,' she said again, flatly. 'He's my husband and he's doing right by me and my son. I think he's wonderful. You should all be very proud of him. Now, if you'll excuse me, I really must go. I'll leave you with Prince Alexandros—he can answer any more questions you might think of. Good evening.'

'Can we have a photograph of the three of you together?' the cameraman pleaded. 'One?'

'Okay.'

Alex was too bemused to protest. Mia would never have agreed to a photograph like this, he thought, but Lily seemed unperturbed. How many photographs had been taken of her today? Obviously one more wasn't going to do any harm.

She turned and stood beside him, holding her son. She smiled.

'Can you lift Prince Michales a little higher?' the cameraman called and Alex thought, damn this, he was going to be part of this photograph, too.

He took Michales from Lily's arms and he held him between them.

Michales gave an indignant squeal, twisted and grabbed for his mother.

He caught the tail of her scarf. And pulled.

Maybe if her hair hadn't been wet he wouldn't have seen. But her hair was tugged upward with the scarf.

For a moment, before the curls fell again, he saw a scar.

A huge scar—from behind her ear almost to her crown.

The photographers hadn't seen. But Lily… She knew he'd seen it. Her face stilled.

Don't say anything, her face said. Please…

He didn't.

In one fluid movement he was tight against her, blocking the reporters' view, twisting her to face the camera slightly side on. So the scar was invisible.

He was holding her close, as if he cared.

Hell, he did care. Why hadn't he asked. *Why hadn't he asked?*

He forced a smile. The photograph was taken. He handed Michales back to Lily—still standing as close as he could. He took the scarf from Michales's chubby fingers and tied it gently around his mother's curls.

'I'll not have you sunburned,' he growled.

'It's almost dusk. There's no need to fear sunburn,' the reporter said.

'No matter. It's time you went up to the house, Lily,' he said and gave her a gentle push.

She got the message. She gave the reporters a brief smile and turned and trudged up the beach. Leaving three men gazing after her. Two reporters who thought they'd just gained a scoop.

One Prince who felt ill.

She'd called him honourable, wonderful even…

He didn't feel either.

'You look confused,' one of the reporters said. He tried to get his face under control again. He was watching Lily walk up the beach. What the hell…?

'You look like you'd like to bed her again,' the man said.

Enough. There was only so much a man could take and this was well over the boundary.

'Excuse me,' he said coldly. 'This is a private beach. You have no right to land here. I think we've given you enough. Can you please leave now?'

'We're going,' the man said and then he hesitated. 'She's a bit different from her sister, then?'

This was where he should turn haughty, supercilious, as if reporters were somewhere beneath pond scum. This was where he should produce a dose of royal arrogance.

He couldn't do it. Not when they were saying something he agreed with so entirely.

'Do you think I'd have married her if she was like Mia?' he demanded.

The reporter hesitated. He looked as if he wanted to say something and finally decided he might as well.

'We came here on the spur of the moment,' he said. 'We never dreamed of getting this close. The old King and his bride…they never let us near.'

That was what he should have done, Alex thought. He knew he needed to protect Lily. Standing on the beach, watching Lily's departing back, the reporters with bare feet and soggy trousers, Alex in his swim shorts and bare chest… It didn't feel like a them-against-us situation. It felt like three guys admiring a cute woman. Three men thinking about how this situation affected the country.

'You know what the headlines are going to be tomorrow?' the reporter asked, still not taking his eyes from the departing Lily. 'They're going to be: "Don't Call Me Ma'am. Call Me Lily." I just figured the angle. A Princess of the People. As a question. Like we need to get to know her before we pass judgement. You want to add anything to that?'

'I don't think I do,' he said, thinking maybe that was where he'd gone wrong in the first place. *We need to get to know her before we pass judgement…*

'You want us to say you threatened to throw us off the beach?'

'I want you to say I'll do anything in my power to protect my own.'

'Nice,' the guy said, grinning and scribbling himself a note. 'Now, all you need to say is that you fell in love with her the first time you saw her…'

'For our women readers,' the younger guy said apologetically. 'They want a love story.'

'I'm not buying into that,' he snapped.

'You can't keep your eyes off her,' the older guy said.

'Neither can you.'

'Yeah, well…' They watched as Lily rounded the last curve in the path and disappeared. There was a communal sigh of regret. 'I expect our readers will add two and two…'

'I hope they will.'

'I'm sure they will,' the reporter said cheerfully. 'We've got some great shots here. You know, if I were you, I'd show her off. You need the rest of the island to take her to their hearts.'

'Just like you have,' the younger reporter said and grinned. 'Can I quote you as saying that, sir?'

CHAPTER NINE

HE'D seen the scar.

No matter, she thought. She'd never consciously hidden her illness from him. If he'd asked, she'd have told him.

But...

But she hated him knowing. That was why she'd consciously played it down, blocking his questions. She hadn't lied to him about it, but neither had she told the truth. For the truth still hurt. The memory of her illness was still terrifying. Even thinking about it—how helpless she'd been—left her feeling exposed. Vulnerable. More vulnerable even than she'd felt getting married, which was really, really vulnerable.

Think about the house, she told herself. Think about practicalities.

Think about anything but Alex.

The house was fabulous.

Lily had spent only a few minutes here while she'd dumped her bridal gear and donned her swimsuit. The beach, the sea, the need to stop being a bride and have a swim, had made her rush. Now she had time to take it in.

Her apartment—a guest wing?—was beautiful: a long, wide room with three sets of French windows opening to the balcony and the sea beyond. The windows were open, the soft curtains floating in the breeze.

Everywhere she looked there were flowers. The boundaries between house and garden were almost indistinguishable.

Fabulous.

So think fabulous, she told herself.

Don't think about Alex.

Was he still at the beach?

Maybe he'd only caught a glimpse of the scar. Maybe he wouldn't ask.

She showered with Michales in her arms. When she emerged, wrapped in one vast fluffy towel, and Michales enclosed in another, birds were doing acrobatics in the vines on the balcony. Finches? Tiny and colourful, they made her feel as if she'd wandered into a fairy tale.

'But this is real,' she told Michales a trifle breathlessly. 'Paradise.'

With Alex?

She thought of his face when he'd seen the scar. He'd looked...numb.

At least she had something she needed to focus on other than Alex's reaction. Michales was drooping. The little boy had been wide-eyed since their arrival, crowing in delight at the sea, soaking it in with all the delight at his small person's disposal. Now he was rubbing his eyes, snuggling against her and beginning to whimper.

He needed to be fed and put to bed. She needed to find the kitchen. She should have checked she had what she needed before she'd gone for a swim, she thought ruefully. She needed to dress fast, but if she put him down he was going to wail.

There was a knock on the door. It swung open—and there was Alex.

He'd moved faster than she had. Showered and dressed, he looked slick and handsome and casually in control of his world.

He was carrying one of Michales's bottles. Filled.

How did he know what was needed?

'I watched the nursery staff feed him a few times before you took him away,' he told her before she asked. 'I know he's a man who doesn't like to be kept from his meals. We knew your formula and…'

'We?'

'Me and my hundred or so staff,' he said and smiled, and she was suddenly far too aware of being dressed in only a towel, which was none too secure.

She was none too secure.

'Why don't you dress while I feed him?' he said and held out his hands to take his son, and that made her feel even more insecure.

'He'll need it warmed.'

'It's already warmed.'

'By your hundred or so staff?'

'Only me here,' he said apologetically. 'A housekeeper comes here every morning, and a gardener when I'm away. When I'm here the gardener doesn't come. That's it.'

'So you live here all by yourself?'

'I do,' he said gravely, then sat on the bed, settled Michales on his knee and offered him his bottle. Michales took it as if he hadn't seen food for days.

'Greedy,' Alex said and chuckled, and Lily felt her insides do that somersaulting thing again and thought she really had to get a grip.

Her towel slipped a bit and she got a grip. Fast.

'I'll get dressed,' she said and grabbed a bunch of clothes and headed for the bathroom.

But she kept the door open. Just a little. There was so much she wanted to know. And it might buy her time. Maybe it could even deflect questions from the scar.

Asking questions could be seen as a pre-emptive strike. Yeah, right, as if that would succeed. But there was little else she could think of to do.

'How long have you had this place?' she called.

'My father had it built when he married my mother.'

'He planted the garden?'

'He and my mother did the basics. My father died when I was five and my mother was forced to leave. My mother and I rebuilt the garden when she came back.' His voice softened. 'She was passionate about gardening. Like you are about boats.'

She'd been steering the conversation to him. There was no way she'd let him deflect the conversation straight back.

'Your mother died when you were…seventeen?'

'Almost seventeen. She was sick for a long time before that.'

'You told me you were raised in the royal nursery.'

'I was,' he said, latent anger suddenly in his voice. 'My uncle hated my father and when I was born that hatred turned… vindictive. Giorgos holds…held…the titles to the entire island. When my father died he banished my mother from the island. Because I was heir to the throne, he demanded I stay.'

'He loved you?'

'He hated me. But if I was to be his heir, he'd control me.'

'Oh, Alex.'

'Yeah, it was tough,' he said. 'The law supported him, and my mother's pleas were ignored. My pleas were ignored.'

'But…you got her back?'

'I did,' he said and she heard a note of grim satisfaction enter his voice. 'Finally. By the time I was fifteen…well, even by fifteen I'd learned things Giorgos didn't want me to know. I was making his life uncomfortable, and he no longer wanted me at the castle. So finally my mother was allowed to return and he allocated an allowance for us to live on. We came back here to live, for all the time she had left.'

There was an untold story here, she knew. A fifteen-year-old standing up to a King. But instinctively she knew he wouldn't tell her more.

'I'm so sorry,' she said.

'There's no need.'

She was still in the bathroom. She had her clothes on now. Jeans, T-shirt.

There was no reason for standing in the bathroom any longer.

She walked out, cautious. Michales had finished his bottle. Her son was looking up at Alex, sleepy but expectant. Alex was looking at Lily, expectant.

The resemblance was unnerving. She was unnerved.

She smiled. It was impossible not to smile at these two.

Her men.

The thought was weird.

'Tell me about your illness,' Alex said softly and her smile died, just like that.

'You don't need to know.'

'I do.' His gaze met hers. Calm. Firm. Unyielding.

The time for dissembling was past.

Okay, then. There was, indeed, no practical reason for her to dissemble—apart from increasing her vulnerability—and she felt so vulnerable anyway she might as well toss in a bit more to the mix.

'I had a brain tumour,' she said, so quickly, so softly that she wasn't sure he'd hear. But the flash of horror in his eyes told her he had.

'A brain tumour…'

'Benign.' The last thing she wanted from this man was sympathy, but sympathy was in his eyes, right from the start, wanted or not. There was also horror.

When the doctors had told her the diagnosis she'd gone to the Diamond Isles to talk to Mia. She'd been hoping for something. Support? Love? Even kindness would have done. But of course Mia had been caught up in her own world. 'Don't be ridiculous,' she'd said when Lily had tried to tell her. 'You've always had your stupid headaches. I won't even begin to think you're right.'

She'd been bereft, lost, foundering. Calls to her mother had gone unanswered. She'd never felt so alone in her life.

Then came the night of the ball. She might as well attend, she'd thought, rather than sit in her bedroom and think about a future that terrified her.

And so she'd met Alex. When Alex had smiled at her, when he'd asked her to dance, she'd found herself falling into his arms. Doing a Mia for once. Living for the moment.

And for two glorious days he'd made her forget reality. He'd smiled at her and she'd let herself believe that all could be right in her world. She'd blocked out the terror. She'd lost herself in his smile, in his laughter, in his loving...

And in his body.

And now here he was, looking at her as if he really cared, and she was lost all over again.

She couldn't be lost. Not when her world was so close to being whole again.

'I always had it,' she said, still too fast, searching for the quickest way to tell him what he had to know. 'Okay, potted history. You probably know my father was a Scottish baronet, a childless widower. My mother was a distant relation of the Greek royal family, fearsomely ambitious. She set her cap at my father's money and title, even though he was forty years her senior. Mia and I were born, two years apart.'

'I know this. The country's been told this.'

'Yes, but as Mia's story. This is mine.'

'Okay,' he said, cradling the almost sleeping Michales. His eyes never left her face. 'You want to sit down and tell me the rest?'

She cast him a scared look. Scared and resentful. Sure she wouldn't be believed.

'No one's pushing you into a chair,' he said gently. 'There's no naked bulb swinging eerily above your head as you spill state secrets. Just tell me.'

She nodded. She closed her eyes. She opened them again

and somehow found the strength to say what needed to be said. 'When I was six I started getting headaches,' she told him. 'I was diagnosed with a tumour, benign but inoperable.' She shrugged. 'I guess that was the end of my parents' marriage. My mother loathed that I was sickly. It was almost an insult— that any daughter of hers could be less than perfect. And then Dad's money ran out.'

She paused. This was too much information. Dumb.

She didn't want this man's sympathy.

Alex's silence scared her, but she had to go on.

'So my mother left, taking Mia with her. Dad and I muddled through as best we could. When Dad died my mother's uncle, a man as different from my mother as it was possible to be— took me in. He was a boat-builder in Whitby in the north of England, and I learned my passion for boats from him. When he died, Spiros, my uncle's friend, persuaded me to go to the States and work for him. So that's what I did. My headaches were a nuisance I'd learned to live with. I made great boats. I was…content.'

'You didn't come to Mia's wedding.'

'I wasn't invited. We'd hardly seen each other since our parents separated and, believe me, I wasn't fussed. Would you have liked to be Mia's bridesmaid?'

She tried a smile then, but she didn't get one in return. His gaze made her feel he was trying to see straight through her. It left her feeling so exposed she was terrified.

Get on, she told herself. Just say it.

'Then the headaches got worse,' she said, trying to get to the point where Alex could stop looking…like he scared her. 'I was getting increasingly dizzy. Increasingly sick. Finally I had tests. The doctors told me the tumour had grown. They thought…unless there was a miracle I had less than a year to live.'

His eyes widened in shock. 'Lily!' His hand reached out towards her but she shook her head. She stepped even further back.

No contact. Not now.

'So I was in a mess,' she said, trying to sound brisk and clinical and knowing by the look on his face she was failing. 'My mother didn't want to know about me. I didn't want to burden Spiros. You've already figured his boatshed looks prosperous but it's struggling. But I had to talk to someone. So, stupidly, I came to the palace to try to talk to Mia. I arrived just in time for the King's celebrations to mark forty years on the throne. That's when I met you.'

Her words had the power to change his world. That was how he felt. As if his world had shifted.

The first time they'd met they'd been surrounded by glittering royalty, the royal ball in full swing. Giorgos had been flaunting his young glamorous wife, taunting him. Telling him there was no way he'd inherit the throne.

But as his uncle had walked past Lily the King's corset had creaked. Lily's lips had twitched. They had, it seemed, a shared sense of the ridiculous.

Intrigued, he'd asked her to dance.

She'd laughed about the chandeliers. She'd gently mocked his tuxedo.

She'd felt like a breath of wind against his heart.

That was the start. They'd laughed and talked for two days. They'd become as close as two people could get.

That she'd had this threat hanging over her…

'So…' He was struggling to find his voice.

'So I slept with you.' Her chin tilted upward in that wonderful, defiant way he was learning to know. 'It was crazy, but crazy was how I felt that night. Crazy wonderful. Yes, we took precautions but maybe I wasn't as careful as I should have been. It was like nothing was real.'

She smiled then, a real smile, with real humour. Making him

remember why he'd wanted her. Making him remember why he'd thought she was different. 'It's okay,' she said softly. 'It was great that night. It was fantastic.'

He didn't feel like smiling. *'I wasn't as careful as I should have been,'* she'd said. How careful had he been?

Not careful enough.

'I got you pregnant.'

She nodded. 'You can't imagine how I felt when I found out. I couldn't work. I had no money. I was having a baby and the headaches were getting more and more frequent. Nevertheless, even after I phoned you… I couldn't consider abortion. I had tests and it was a little boy and he was so real. I wanted… I so wanted…'

She shook her head, seemingly shaking away a memory that held nothing but despair. Moving on. 'Well, finally I contacted Mia again,' she whispered. 'She gave me the same dumb line. It was my business. Not hers. But then she phoned back. Excited. It seemed Giorgos was infertile. They'd been quietly trying to arrange an adoption, but they'd so much rather it was my baby. I know her reasons now—Giorgos's reasons. But by then I was so sick I couldn't enquire and even if I'd known maybe I wouldn't have cared. All I could think was that Mia would give my baby a chance of life.'

He didn't respond. The audacity of the scheme still left him dumbfounded. Mia and Giorgos using Lily's desperation for their own ends… How could Lily have guessed their intention?

And of course Lily had accepted their offer. It was the child's best chance. In a royal household, she knew the baby would at least be well taken care of. Like Lily, the alternatives seemed unbearable.

He looked down at the almost sleeping Michales. His son. To not bring this little boy into the world… The child of two mature parents, conceived in what could almost be taken as love…

He thought again of the call she'd made to him in early pregnancy, and of his response, and he felt sick.

There was a drawn-out silence. Silence and silence and more silence.

She hated it. He could see it. She hated anyone knowing, but to tell him... It was making her feel exposed and frightened and very, very small.

'But you survived?' he said softly, finally, into the stillness.

'So I did,' she said humourlessly. 'You think I'm lying?'

'I didn't say that.' He shook his head. Definite. 'My God, Lily...' Once again he put a hand out towards her but she backed even further. Standing against the French windows as if preparing to flee.

'Let me finish.' She hesitated, then forced herself to go on. 'Part of this I've only heard from others,' she said. 'But I need to tell you. Mia and Giorgos paid for me to be admitted to a private hospital in France, a place known for its discretion. Mia arrived as I was getting really ill. I know now that her plan was to tell the people back on the Diamond Isles that she was pregnant and suffering complications. If my baby survived to term she'd take him as hers. Giorgos would bribe anyone who needed to be bribed.'

'But how did she...?'

'I can't tell you what I don't know,' she said bluntly. 'I gather I ended up in a coma. I gather Michales was born. I also gather one of the nurses in the hospital became really troubled that I was lying untreated. Apparently, until Michales was born, Mia acted concerned, but after she took him I was left alone.' She took a deep breath. 'The nurse saved my life. She risked her job and contacted a doctor she knew who was doing groundbreaking surgery. He checked me out and figured he had nothing to lose if he tried operating. Mia had left my mother's contact details for when I died. The surgeon contacted her for permission to operate—offering to do it for free.' She managed a smile again. 'Even my mother couldn't knock that back. So finally I woke. The tumour was gone. Unbelievably gone. I had my life.'

He didn't know what to say. He just gazed at her in awe.

'Unreal, isn't it?' she said, half mocking. 'Unbelievable. Parts of it I didn't figure out myself until I arrived here at your coronation, and even now I'm having trouble coming to terms with it. But it's okay. I'm not asking for belief. I'm not asking for anything. I just want to build boats and care for my son. I want to live.'

Her chin tilted forward again, pugnacious, defensive.

How could he believe such a story?

But then he thought of Mia. He'd been present at the wedding, and he remembered Mia's mother as well. They were two of a kind. Grasping, greedy, social climbers. Flaunting their connection to the Greek royal family and to English aristocracy.

They were about as different from this woman as it was possible to be.

'I won't impinge on your freedom,' he said softly and she nodded.

'Good, then.'

'But…no one came near you?'

'Spiros and Eleni would have if I'd told them. I didn't tell them.'

'I would have if you'd let me.'

'Would you?'

'You can believe it. It's true. Hell, Lily, you could have died.'

'That's what I expected,' she said. 'I guess nothing will ever be so bad again. Drifting into unconsciousness, knowing there was no return ticket. Knowing I had to leave my baby in Mia's care.'

'If I could get my hands on her…'

'There's no joy down that road,' she said simply. 'Being angry just makes everything worse. Anyway…' she shrugged '…now you know. We can get on with it.'

'With what?'

'With our sham marriage. With doing what we have to do before I can go home.'

'Where's home?'

'Where Michales is,' she said simply. 'I don't care about places. I care about my baby. That's all.'

CHAPTER TEN

SHE'D lied.

I care about my baby. That's all. She'd known it was a lie before she'd uttered it but she wasn't about to add her other…care.

Alex.

He looked appalled. It helped, she decided, that he looked appalled at what she'd gone through. When she let herself think about it, she was pretty appalled herself.

That he was horrified on her behalf… It did something to her insides. There was a warmth forming inside her—a glow that was starting to build.

She looked down at the bed, where he still sat holding Michales on his knee.

Her men.

Her family.

She'd never had family. Her mother had been entirely uninterested in her sickly daughter. Her father had been elderly when she was born and their relationship had been built on Lily's role as carer. Mia simply didn't want to be a part of her life.

But here…this man didn't want her to care for him, she thought.

This man cared.

Um…no. He'd been horrified at an appalling story. Nothing more.

So don't get your hopes up, she told herself severely.

Michales was starting to grizzle. After his swim and shower and feed he should be drifting into sleep.

So be a mother, she reminded herself sharply.

She lifted Michales from Alex's arms, held him to her shoulder and rubbed his back.

He emitted one very satisfactory belch.

Alex's brows hiked in amazement. 'Is he supposed to do that?'

As an ice breaker it was great. The tension inside the room fizzled and died, and she found she could smile, too.

'Better out than in, wouldn't you say?' She was laying Michales into his cot. He'd had a very busy day for a baby. A wedding, a reception, a first ever swim… He snuggled down, his eyes closing almost before he was tucked in.

She stood gazing down at him. When she looked up, Alex was standing beside her.

The tension zoomed in again.

'What?' she said, suddenly breathless.

'You're beautiful,' he said on a note of discovery.

'Yeah, dressed to kill.' Jeans and T-shirt. Her standard uniform for life. She'd left the scarf off. Why bother?

'Lily…'

'Let's not,' she managed.

'Not what?'

'Whatever you're about to say. Like paying compliments. I don't like it.'

'You don't like compliments?'

'Mia gets the compliments. You want Mia? You need to line up behind a guy called Ben.'

'You're nothing like Mia.'

'Well, there's the truth. Can you excuse me? I need to unpack.' She made to go past him but his hands caught her shoulders and held.

'Lily, can we start again?'

'I don't know what you mean.'

'Wind the clock back,' he said softly. 'So we don't have baggage between us.'

'By baggage I guess you mean Michales.'

'He's very noisy baggage,' he said and smiled as he glanced into the cot. 'I doubt he fits the description. But in a way…he complicates things. Your illness complicates things. All sorts of things complicate…things.'

'What do you mean?'

'Between you and me.'

'There's nothing…'

'You see, that's where we differ.' He moved so he had a hand on each arm. His hands were on her bare skin. They felt big and warm and sure. In his hold she suddenly felt…safe.

'Alex, don't,' she murmured but still he held her, his eyes asking questions.

'Don't what?'

'H-hold me.'

'You don't want to be held?'

'I'm scared.' It wasn't true, but it was what she ought to feel. She should be running a mile. But she could give herself to him.

The idea was suddenly there, and it was so overwhelming that *scared* was the right description. To give herself to this man…

She'd married him, she thought, frantically trying to get her hormones under control. But to fall in love with him… To give her heart…

She already had.

Sensations were sweeping in from all sides.

And suddenly she was remembering how she'd felt during those last appalling months, as the tumour in her head had threatened to overwhelm her. She'd had times when she was dazed, confused, disoriented. The sensation of being out of control was terrifying.

Gazing at Alex now, that was how she felt. As if her body wasn't her own. As if her head wasn't her own.

'Lily, what is it?' He was gazing at her in concern. Something of what she was feeling must have shown in her face, for the grip of his hands changed. It was a subtle shift. Not a withdrawal exactly but… From the beginnings of passion, it had changed to a hold of comfort. 'Lily, I won't hurt you.'

'I know you won't.' But here was a shift again. She didn't want him to look like that. She didn't want this man's sympathy.

The night Michales had been conceived had been a night out of frame. She'd emerged from plain, frightened Lily to being someone else. She'd been seductive, wild and free.

It had been imaginary.

It had been fun.

The memory of that fun was with her now, like an itch building within. Goading her. Go on, Lily. You know you can be like that again. If you dare…

'Alex, are you suggesting…that you want this marriage for real?' she whispered.

'What do you mean?'

'I know it's not love at first sight or anything like that,' she said hurriedly. 'But we've…we've got this attraction thing going.'

'We do.' He sounded puzzled, but laughter was replacing sympathy. Which was what she wanted—wasn't it?

No. She wanted a serious discussion.

'I'd prefer it if you didn't laugh,' she told him, and he schooled his expression to gravity.

'Of course. I'm not laughing. So you're saying we might be attracted to one another. I agree. So where might that be taking us?'

'See, here's the thing,' she said, fighting for courage. But suddenly she was sure she was right. Mia wasn't the only one who could fight for what she wanted, she thought. All her life she'd let events shape her course. Now…she had her life back.

She had a beautiful baby, and before her was the most gorgeous prince in the known universe and he was her husband. Whatever the reason for the marriage, marriage it clearly was.

So here was the idea. What was the harm in asking for more?

'When we made our wedding vows, did you mean any of them?' she asked quickly, before any more qualms raised their heads.

'You mean keeping me only unto you for as long as we both shall live?' he asked, and the laughter in his eyes had suddenly gone. 'Lily…'

She hadn't meant to get this serious; it was scary. 'I didn't mean that,' she said hurriedly. 'I wouldn't ask that. For as long as we both shall live… This is only for a year. And you've known me for what—two minutes?'

'I've known you for over a year.'

'But in real time. Two days and a couple of meetings in between. Not enough to base a whole life on. But what I'm asking…' She faltered, fought to find the right words and then forced herself to say them. 'It's just the first bit. It's the keeping yourself only unto me.'

'Keeping myself faithful to you, do you mean?'

He had it. She nodded, relieved it was in the open. 'That's the one.'

'Are you suggesting you might want to keep a couple of gigolos on the side while we're married?' It was said lightly but his gaze said this wasn't a light question. His gaze was locked onto hers, as if he were trying to see inside her.

'Of course I don't,' she said. Unconsciously her chin tilted again, assertive. Or trying to be assertive. Inside, she was jelly. 'Alex, I'm willing to swear that for the whole time I'm married to you I will be faithful.' Deep breath. Just ask, she told herself. Do it. And she did. 'Will you do the same for me?'

And there was no hesitation at all. 'I will,' he said, and he might as well have said *I do*, there was such gravitas.

Her eyes widened. Just like that, she had his promise.

She didn't know where to take it from here.

He was watching her, concerned now by her silence. 'You don't believe me?'

'It's just…you're a royal prince, you could have anyone. I didn't think you'd want to be…'

'Monogamous?'

'That's the one.' She was practically stuttering. She felt as if she was tying herself in knots. 'What makes you different?'

'I wouldn't mind seeing if it works,' he said, so softly she thought at first she'd got it wrong. But the way he was looking at her said she had it exactly right.

I wouldn't mind seeing if it works… That was an implication that he wanted something more than a marriage of convenience.

Don't go there, she thought. She wasn't ready. She wanted her freedom. Or she thought she did. Alex was…fabulous. But to be sucked into the royal goldfish bowl for ever…

Think about that later, she told herself. Later was truly scary. Think about here. Think about now.

Right here, right now, her prince was promising to be faithful. To her. While they were married.

Starting now?

'You're beautiful, Lily,' he said softly. 'You've had such a tough time…'

'See, that's just what I don't want you to think,' she snapped, confusion fading. 'That's what I suddenly realised. Last time you took me to bed…did you do it because you felt sorry for me?'

'Of course I didn't.'

'Then that's what I'd like to revert to. I remember lying beside you and thinking it was magic. Thinking your body was scrumptious.'

'Scrumptious,' he said blankly and then he grinned. 'I believe that's what I thought about your body as well,' he said and the laughter had slammed back.

Shared laughter… That was what had attracted her to him in the first place. A whole lot of other sensations had fallen into line behind that initial attraction—a body to die for, sensations like tenderness, passion and wonder. But laughter had come first and it was laughter that was a refuge here. If they could laugh… Scary emotions could be left for later.

She could be free later on. She could be free when she had to be free. For now… Maybe this was dumb, but his sympathy, his concern, had seemed to unlock something inside her that had never been touched. From swearing she wanted to keep her life for herself and for her son, suddenly she was thinking what if…what if…

'So you're promising to keep yourself only unto me all the time we're married,' she ventured.

'I am.' Flat. Definite. Absolute.

'So…' She swallowed. 'If we're to be faithful…'

'Mmm.'

'And if we're to be…chaste…as well, then we might have a very monastic type of year in front of us.'

'I'd make a very bad monk,' he said promptly, laughter returning. He seemed to be willing to go where she was leading. More than willing. 'I don't think a tonsure would suit me.'

She looked up at his thick black curls. She tried to imagine what he'd look like with a neat ring of hair and a bald crown.

She chuckled.

'Not a sexy look,' he said, smiling his agreement, and she smiled back at him. And wham! Here they came again. Hormones and hormones and more hormones.

But there were things to be said—things that must be said if those hormones were allowed to hold sway.

'If…if we were to sleep together we'd need to take a lot more precautions than last time,' she managed, trying not to sound as breathless as she felt.

'I've changed my brand of condom.'

She blinked. He was smiling. He was with her and beyond.

Two could play at that game. 'I've taken precautions, too,' she said, and watched his eyes crease into surprise and appreciation—and then darken to something more.

'You've taken precautions,' he said softly.

'That's what I said.'

'You've taken precautions already?'

'Seeing as I was getting married. Seeing as I didn't trust myself.' Seeing also as she hadn't trusted him not to demand his conjugal rights. She'd never dreamed the advance could come from her.

'I see.' His hands took hers, gripping warmly, strongly, surely, and the laughter was back again. Laughter and something deeper. 'So let me get this right. You're in my house on your wedding night—*our* wedding night—you look so lovely I can't believe it and you tell me you came prepared.'

'That's not necessarily an invitation,' she managed, but of course it was. And he was playing her game.

'It'd be a prince without chivalry who thought it was,' he said and he tugged her closer. 'But if it was a prince who was to issue the invitation…'

'What…what sort of invitation?' she managed.

'A very proper invitation,' he whispered. His mouth was against her hair. She could feel his breath. It was unbelievably erotic. Unbelievably sexy. 'Something like: His Majesty, Prince Alexandros Kostantinos Mykonis, Crown Prince of Sappheiros, requests the pleasure of the company of Her Majesty, Princess Lily Mykonis…'

'Princess…' It was practically a squeak. She swallowed. 'Um…princess?'

'That's what you are as my wife,' he said into her hair. 'Whereas Mia is now Queen of nowhere, as the Kingdom of Diamas no longer exists. She's about to get a very legal letter telling her she has no further right to use the title.'

She gazed at Alex—*at her husband*—in awe. Thinking of Mia's reaction.

'I think you're wonderful,' she said before she could help herself, and the world stood still.

His eyes darkened once more. She saw passion flare and burn. 'So this invitation I'm thinking of issuing…' he murmured.

'When?' she asked, still breathless, but no longer worrying about an irrelevant thing like breathing.

'I'm getting to that,' he said reprovingly. 'Patience, my love. Official invites take time. I need to melt the wax for the seal… Oh, I'll have to find some wax. You don't happen to have a candle about you?'

'I don't believe I do. And I certainly don't have time to search for one.'

'You don't?'

'Not the way I'm feeling.'

'So…' His hold tightened. 'If I were to send this invitation without an official seal… If I were to request an RSVP by return post…'

'You might get it faster than you expected.'

'Really?'

'Really,' she whispered. 'Right about…now.'

'Now?' His hands were in the small of her back, tugging her closer, closer. 'Now, my love?'

'Maybe,' she whispered.

'And what might this RSVP say?'

'Ooh,' she whispered. 'I'd have to think about it.'

'Think fast.'

She thought fast. She could think without breathing. 'I guess it'd say something along the lines of: Her Majesty, Princess Lily Sophia Mykonis, is delighted to receive the very gracious invitation of said prince and accepts with pleasure.'

'Does she just.' She could feel his pleasure. She could feel his heat. The world outside had ceased to exist. There was only each other.

How had they done it? How had they turned a sedate domestic scene—feeding her baby—into passion, just like that?

But there was no mistaking what had happened. Her knees felt distinctly wobbly, but there was no longer a need for them to stay firm. Alex was sweeping her up into his arms, holding her against him, his dark eyes possessing her, loving her, wanting her.

Her prince.

'About place and time…' he murmured.

'Subject to negotiation, wouldn't you say?'

'Okay, let's negotiate. First factor—time. Is now okay with you?'

'I don't believe I have any pressing appointments.'

'Excellent.' His dark eyes gleamed. 'Place?'

'Maybe not here,' she said, somewhat reluctantly.

'We might corrupt our son,' he said, and those two words…*our son*…were so sexy that her insides felt quivery along with her knees. All of her felt quivery.

'See that adjoining door?' he murmured, and she looked up and saw the door and her eyes widened.

'You don't mean…'

'I do mean.' He was laughing again. She loved it when he laughed.

'You had this planned!'

'I did not,' he said, wounded. 'But, as a good father, I thought I might be expected to take a turn at night duty. I thought if I was to lie awake at night listening for my son then I'd need to be near. Really near. So I allocated you this apartment.'

'You're saying your bed is right through that door?'

'Right through that door. If it's grand enough for you.'

'I can make do,' she said serenely. 'But I don't mind a bit of glitz. The last time I… The last time we made love, I believe you were sleeping at the castle. Under a chandelier, if I re-member correctly.'

'I was there as my uncle's heir,' he said. 'He liked glitz. He also expected me to act as his deputy, so I was on duty.'

'But you're not on duty now.'

'I'm delegating responsibility to my son.' He grinned. 'I like the idea of delegating. If there's armed insurrection before the morning, Michales is responsible for waking me up and ringing the newspapers.'

She choked.

'I love it when you laugh,' he whispered and it was so much what she was thinking that she gasped.

'What?' he demanded.

'I guess...laughter from you is a real turn-on as well,' she admitted.

'You like it when I laugh?'

'I love it when you laugh.'

'So we should find ourselves a good piece of slapstick on television?'

'We could,' she said cautiously.

'But I can think of something better,' he growled and he walked across and kicked the door open. It wasn't even properly closed, Lily thought, and she couldn't figure whether she was shocked or delighted.

But then she thought again. Definitely delighted. For Alex was carrying her across to his bed and laying her on the counterpane as if she were the most exquisite thing he'd ever touched.

'I'm sorry there's no chandelier,' he whispered.

'I can cope. As long as there's laughter,' she said, breathless again. When he looked like that...

It was still too soon, the sane part of her brain whispered. Sense said she needed to taste freedom first.

But not now. Not when the rest of her brain was disagreeing. Not as he was tugging his shirt free, baring his chest, making her gasp…

'Laughter,' he said, agreeing. Smiling and smiling. 'Okay, my love, here we go. Two sausages in a pan. One turns to the other and says, "Gee, it's hot in here." What does the other one say?'

He was loving her with his eyes. He was smiling down at her with that wicked, laughing smile—and he was waiting for an answer to his dumb riddle. 'I don't know,' she whispered, choking with laughter and something else entirely. 'What does the other one say?'

'"Bless my soul, it's a talking sausage!"' he said, and he grinned like a seven-year-old cracking his first riddle. It was so ridiculous she found herself laughing with him.

While hungering for him with every nerve in her body.

And then he was beside her on the bed, lifting her T-shirt over her head. Unclipping her bra.

'But it's not just the sausage who's hot,' he whispered, laughter fading, his strong, skilful fingers moving to cup her breasts. 'Lily, you're the most beautiful woman in the world. You give yourself to me and I can't believe that you do. I'll never let you forget it. But now, my love… Now is for us. Now is for laughter. Now is for loving. And if we try very hard…' He closed his eyes and she had a feeling he was taking a mighty step forward. 'Now might just end up being forever.'

Only forever had a habit of being not as long as expected.

In Athens, a plane was landing. A private jet. A woman emerged. She stood on the tarmac and surveyed the scene before her. Deeply displeased.

There was no one to meet her. Olivia had needed to barter with her daughter to get this flight. Mia had grudgingly arranged for Ben's plane to bring her here. The negotiations had made her seethe. While her daughters lived in splendour, she had to fend for herself.

Okay, maybe she would have done the same if she'd been her daughters' age, she conceded. Maybe she had. But for Lily to forget she was her mother… Not even to invite her to her wedding…

Some things were unconscionable. Sometimes a gentle reminder was needed.

Or a big one.

She made her way into the terminal, went through Customs—like a mere mortal, she thought savagely—and then thought of what to do next.

A private plane to Sappheiros was out of the question. Unless…

Unless the press came to the party. Which they would. She simply had to open her mouth and tell them who she was.

Mother of the Queen. Mother of the Crown Princess.

She'd done very well for her girls.

She now intended Lily to acknowledge it.

CHAPTER ELEVEN

FOR three days he made her laugh, he made her love, he made her live.

She'd never felt so alive. She'd never thought life could be so magical.

She wasn't to know that Alex had posted guards to prevent more intrusions into the little cove beneath the house. There were roadblocks set up to stop intrusions from the road. She thought this was normal, this was what life could be like, married to this man and living happily ever after.

And he was learning to love his son.

Of all the seductive turn-ons, this was the most powerful. For Alex's delight—his infatuation and wonder with his infant son— were impossible to disguise. He made Michales laugh, and every time he did she fell deeper and deeper in love with him. He swam with Michales in his arms, and she watched them and ached with happiness. She loved it that when Michales murmured it was Alex who'd scoop up the little boy and bring him back to their bed. He'd heat his bottle and they'd feed him together, and then Alex would take him back to his cot and tuck him in.

He told his son stories. She wasn't supposed to hear—he thought she was sleeping—but she lay and listened to him telling Michales all about this island, all the things they could do, all that life offered.

When Michales wouldn't settle they lay and told each other stories of their past. They were telling Michales of his history, they said solemnly to each other, but in reality they were growing closer and closer to each other.

She learned of Alex's childhood. She learned of the aching void left by his father's death, the desperation when his mother had to leave the island, leaving him with an uncle he loathed.

She even heard briefly of his desperation when his mother died. He skimmed over it but she heard enough to know he'd cared for her on his own, that Giorgos had let no one come near, that her death had changed who he was for ever.

He'd been known as a man who walked alone. She understood it now—a little. A tiny part of her was starting to think that maybe she could change it.

But now wasn't for resolutions. Now was simply for…now. For listening and learning and loving.

She learned of his friendship with Nikos and Stefanos. The 'guardians', they'd called themselves, and it seemed they might now all be in power; they'd hold government of each of these, the Diamond Isles. They had plans.

She listened to those plans. Alex could achieve them now. He lay beside her, he played with his son, he let his big body curve against hers and he told her his ideas for financial restructure, economic growth, tourism, wealth for this island he loved so much.

The stories weren't one-way. In turn he probed her childhood. He grew silent as she told him, and she knew his silence was anger. The sensation was incredible. No one had ever been angry on her behalf.

Her mother had deserted her. Her father had leaned on her, and her sister… Well, Mia was to be forgotten.

'Though I'd love to think of something else we could do,' Alex murmured. 'Stripping her of her title isn't enough. That she left you for dead…'

Michales had just been fed. Cradled between his mother and his father, he was sliding fast towards sleep, with the look of one very contented baby.

When he went to sleep… Lily was already tingling in anticipation of what would happen when he went to sleep.

She needed not to think about that, she told herself, trying to be severe. She needed to listen to what Alex was saying.

'I'm thinking of some sort of permanent memorial,' he said. 'We're opening a new refuse station on the far side of the island. How about we call it the Mia and Giorgos Garbage Dump? By royal decree.'

She grinned. 'You're a wonderful man, Alexandros.'

'I know,' he said humbly. He looked at Michales. The baby's eyes were closed. 'Our baby's asleep,' he said with deep satisfaction.

'Well, then…'

'You want to make love or go for a swim?'

'I…'

'More indecision,' he said and sighed. 'There are royal decrees all over the place this morning. Okay then, here's another. Lovemaking. Followed by swim. Followed by more lovemaking. And later… I intend to make you dinner.'

It was a dream time. It was a time of wonder but it had to end. He could ill afford three days. The island's grim financial situation couldn't wait any longer. There were decisions everywhere that needed his attention.

He had to leave.

He couldn't bear to tell Lily this had to end, but end it must.

He'd use this last night to good effect, he decided. He wouldn't talk about leaving.

Up until now they'd lived on what was in the refrigerator. His staff had stocked it well, but it was all ready-made stuff. He'd told his housekeeper to stay away. But this night had to be special.

When had she had someone cook for her? Never, he thought.

In the afternoons she'd taken to sleeping with Michales. She hadn't taken the time she needed after the operation to let her body recover fully, he thought. He insisted she take it now.

She thought he slept beside her, but instead he lay and watched them.

His wife. His son.

They slept while he watched over them.

Things were changing inside him. He was acknowledging a hunger he hadn't known he had until it was being assuaged.

His wife. His son.

So on this, the last day of their honeymoon, he left them while she slept and headed into the town.

She woke as he was unpacking in the kitchen, and came to investigate the sounds.

'Dinner,' he said, smiling at her, his beautiful wife, dressed in only a loose sarong. His beautiful Princess. 'I've decided you need feeding and it's time I lent a hand.'

'I can feed myself.'

'Not tonight.' He flipped her a disc and motioned to the sound system. 'Here's our music. You listen while I cook.'

So she sat and played with Michales and watched her husband cook her dinner.

He took over the whole kitchen. He was so large. So overpoweringly male.

So wonderful?

He upended a bag. Fat, juicy scallops with their lips still intact spilled out onto the table in a luscious heap.

Since her illness she'd been having trouble eating. Trauma, depression, shock—she didn't know what had caused it. She had to eat, but she couldn't remember a time when she'd last felt hungry.

She suddenly felt really, really hungry. And really, really…

Hungry, she thought again, but not for food.

Alex was piling the scallops into a bowl and unpacking the next parcel. Coriander, Lily thought, smelling the pungent herb. Mmm.

'Would you mind not looking like that?' he demanded.

'Like what?'

'You know very well like what,' he said. 'Like I need to sweep you up and carry you back to my bedroom right now. Or take you right here, among the coriander. But no. I'm a man on a mission. No distractions, woman. Listen to the music and let your Prince of the Kitchen do what he's here for. That's an order.'

He was setting out to make her smile and make her eat. Life had been bleak for this woman for a long time but right now, if he tried hard enough, he could make her smile.

He'd brought Abba. She'd put on the disc expecting—what—something classical? But instead there was Benny and Bjorn and Agnetha and Frida belting out their toe-tapping harmonies with passion. He could practically feel their Lycra.

It was impossible for her not to smile as she toe-tapped with Abba.

He cooked the scallops, searing them fast, then serving them on lettuce cups with a light dressing of coriander and lemon. Lily ate six while she listened to 'Dancing Queen'.

He watched her eat in quiet satisfaction. This was what he'd set out to do—have her eat without thinking about it.

Maybe she was thinking about the food, but the whole setting was confounding. He could see that. Him. His cooking. The music.

Excellent.

He would have liked to give her a really hefty steak as the next course, but in the end he'd opted for temptation rather than substance. So, instead of steak, he served slivers of fish caught that morning, coated in tempura batter and lightly fried. He accompanied them with tiny potatoes, parboiled and crisped in the oven. A salad of witlof, asparagus, mango and herbs.

'Fernando' started as he served the main course. It was one of Abba's slowest, finest songs and it meant Lily could lose herself in the music and eat again without thinking. She ate three slivers of fish, three tiny potatoes and a good serving of salad.

He cleared the plates with the same satisfaction he might have felt if his company received top place in the Chelsea Flower Show.

She seemed…bemused.

She really was beautiful, he thought as he watched her enjoy herself. When he'd first met her he'd thought her hair was glorious. Now, with her mass of drifting curls replaced by an almost boyishly short crop, he thought her hair had been a distraction. Her eyes were huge in her pale face. Her face was alive with emotion and enjoyment as Abba launched into 'Take a Chance on Me'.

Beautiful didn't begin to cut it.

He'd taken this woman to bed. She'd borne his son. He'd married her. Now, weirdly, he was starting to regret it. He'd like to start this again, without the baggage, without the tentative twelve-month time line, without the feeling that she'd been coerced into marrying him.

He'd filled her wineglass but she'd drunk a mere inch. She was still wary, he thought. She was giving in to the moment but she was still…afraid? Maybe that was too harsh a word, but behind her laughter there was always the echo of knowledge that this had to end.

He didn't want her to think this had to end. He didn't want her to be wary. He wanted her to laugh.

He wanted her to be free, he thought. Free to decide to love him?

Would she want a real marriage?

Would she want to be tied to him?

More and more, it was what he wanted. With Lily by his side, he could do anything, he thought. They could change this island together. They could truly be Sappheiros's ruling couple.

The thought was so exhilarating that he wanted to shout it. He wanted to tell her, to hold her in his arms and say it just like he'd thought it.

But he had to be wary here. There were loose ends. He'd left them loose because…because he hadn't wanted to commit himself. Only now he did.

But he wasn't going to pressure her. This was too important to mess with.

And he had things to sort out. He'd leave tomorrow and get it sorted—get it all sorted. Then he'd come back and woo her as she deserved to be wooed.

Meanwhile…dessert. He'd sweated over the dessert, wanting to present her with something irresistible. But the thought of her still pale and thin face had given him pause.

He'd cared for his mother when she'd been ill that last time, and he'd learned a little about invalid appetites. Lily was still recovering. A big dessert, a slab of luscious chocolate cake, for instance, could serve only to make her feel queasy.

He'd learned the hard way that tiny amounts were far more tempting.

So he'd lashed out on a really special dessert. Now he spent ten minutes arranging it, while Lily listened to 'Mamma Mia', 'Rock Me' and 'Take a Chance on Me'.

She didn't talk. The only way to get her to talk was for him to push, but he wouldn't push.

What he was trying to do… Well, to be honest, he was still trying to figure it out for himself, but he knew it behoved him to behave as if he were balancing on eggshells.

This was precious.

That would do as an adjective, he decided. He didn't know what to do with it, but he knew it had to be protected.

Lily.

Michales.

Lily.

His family?

Where was he going?

He knew where he was going. Maybe it scared him, but the alternative was far, far worse.

Family was what he wanted.

The dessert was irresistible. It was served on an antique platter, delicate china etched with faded rosebuds, pink and cream. On the plate…six tiny desserts. A tiny chocolate éclair. A thimbleful of chocolate-orange mousse. Crystallized ginger. A strawberry sponge cake, exquisite in miniature. A gold-burned baked caramel, two spoonfuls at the most. Grapes, frosted with sugar and glistening.

Yum.

Maybe she could relax a bit more, she decided, and took another sip of his lovely wine. Just a little. Just enough to enjoy the desserts.

He'd bought the desserts from the best cook on the island. Marika had had to close her restaurant tonight to prepare them, but what the heck? What was the use of being royal and rich if you couldn't be indulgent? Watching Lily try and resist the last grape—and fail—Alex thought it'd have been worth it if it had cost half his fortune.

She had him fascinated. More.

He'd wanted her the first time he'd seen her, and he wanted her so much now it was like a hunger, starting deep within and refusing to be sated. Wary of commitment for so long, he knew now what the truth was.

He wanted her on whatever terms she cared to name.

She popped the last grape into her mouth and smiled at him. 'All finished. And our son's fast asleep. What to do, what to do…'

'I'll show you,' he told her. And did.

* * *

He needed to get his business over and come back here. They slept in each other's arms but he woke before Lily and gently disentangled himself. He showered and dressed and she woke to find him standing over her with a mug of coffee, toast and an apologetic smile.

She sat up fast, drawing the sheet up to her chin.

She'd changed in these three days, Alex thought. She'd blossomed. She glowed from the inside out.

His Lily. He'd known she was beautiful but he couldn't have guessed how beautiful.

She held his heart in the palm of her hand.

'What do you think you're doing?' She sounded a little bit scared, he thought, but she was covering it with indignation. 'Dressed, sir, when I'm not.'

'A man has to have the advantage some time.'

'Well, I don't like it,' she said. 'Come back to bed.'

'I need to go back to the palace. I have things to do. I may need to make a fast trip to Manhattan.'

Her face stilled. 'Of…of course.'

'Will you stay here until I come back?'

'You'll be back…when?'

'A week? Maybe less. I can't say.'

'As long as that?'

'I can't help it, Lily. There's pressure from all sides. But now that you and Michales are settled…'

Her face grew even more expressionless. 'You've sorted us out and now you can move on?'

'I didn't mean that.' He looked down at her and she was so lovely… He should sit down here and now and tell her his plans. His dreams. His desire to fit her into his life so she'd never leave.

But if she reacted badly… If she took fright… The need to go was imperative, and if she didn't agree… He wouldn't have time to retrieve it.

Better not to say anything until he could return and stay.

And maybe she understood. 'I know you didn't,' she said, contrite, schooling herself to look calm. 'I know you need to go. I need to catch up with Spiros as well. I haven't even seen his boatshed.'

'It's great,' he said, grateful she'd moved on so easily. 'He and Eleni are in a house by the harbour—my people set it up for them. As far as the boatyard goes, Spiros is using a small one for now but in the long-term he'll tell us what he needs and we'll build a bigger one.'

She tried to get her head around this. Alex sounded business-like. She needed to be, too.

Their honeymoon…was over?

'I thought you said this country was poverty-stricken.'

'It is, but if I pay bills and do nothing else we'll be bankrupt in no time. I'm organizing to rationalize our debts and work our way through them. Now I'm Crown Prince I can sell our overseas assets, and I can also access royal funds. I can get Spiros's boatshed working, employing locals, and that's just the beginning. I can get this whole island working.'

He bent and kissed her solidly—so solidly that her coffee slopped onto the sheets. 'Uh-oh,' he said and took her coffee, placed it on the side table and started kissing her again. 'Don't worry about a little stain,' he said. 'We've practically worn this set of sheets out anyway.'

'There's an ego,' she said, and he smiled.

'There's a lot to boast about,' he said. 'You've given me this, Lily. By agreeing to marry me… There's nothing I can't do.'

She smiled at his enthusiasm. But… But… She kissed him back but, for the first time in days, she knew doubt.

By agreeing to marry me…

He could have had all this without marrying her, she thought. Couldn't he?

Maybe not.

Of course not. She knew that.

How could she have forgotten? She'd agreed to marry him to secure the Crown so he could save this country. Not because he wanted to wake up beside her for the rest of her life.

He was moving on. He'd stepped back now, and she saw the latent energy in him, her Prince about to achieve his goals for this nation. He'd achieved what he needed here. It was time to move on to the next challenge.

She was being fanciful, she thought, but she couldn't stop a shiver starting deep and growing.

'Lily, you're beautiful,' he said, sensing her doubt and looking as if he didn't know how to quell it. Looking as if he didn't have time to quell it. 'You know you are. But…' he glanced at his watch and grimaced '…I'm meeting a group of international bankers at the palace in two hours and there are figures I need to check first. I've stayed with you for as long as I can. You'll be okay on your own?'

'Of course.' There was no *of course* about it, but a girl had some pride. 'Go slay 'em, my love.'

'I've organized a car for you. It's in the garage and the keys are on the bench in the kitchen. There's a baby seat in the back for Michales. Go down to the harbour if you want, and find Spiros. Just keep a low profile and stay away from the press.'

'You don't want me talking to the press?'

'It'd be better if we did it together.' He bent to kiss her again—hard, possessive, claiming his own. 'You and I stand together. We're a team. Remember that.'

He touched her lightly on the cheek. He strode into the other room and bent over Michales for a moment—a silent farewell to his son.

And he was gone.

We're a team, Lily repeated softly to herself. A team.

Only…what sort of a team was it when one member was free

to come and go as he pleased? The other…had been told not to speak to the press. Had been given permission to visit Spiros.

He's not promising you a real marriage, she told herself, fighting against sudden, inexplicable desolation. This is a marriage of convenience. The fact that we enjoy each other's bodies…

She enjoyed more than his body.

No. *Enjoy* was such a miserly word.

She loved.

A woman who's ruled by her heart is a fool.

Where had that come from? It was a saying of her mother's. She remembered her mother explaining why she had to leave.

'We've run out of money and your father wants to move to a cottage on the coast. I can't live that life. You say you love your father, but love isn't in my vocabulary. It shouldn't be in yours either. Mia and I are going. Come if you want but don't whinge about your headaches if you do. I can't bear it. And if you stay…don't blame me if you end up unhappy. Make decisions with your head, Lily. A woman who's ruled by her heart is a fool.'

Maybe she was a fool. She was so deeply in love.

What was she doing?

She rose and crossed to the windows looking over the driveway. Alex was driving a Jeep. Until now she hadn't even known he had a car here.

Her sense of unease deepened.

And then…as his Jeep approached the rhododendron drive she saw two men in suits step out of the shadows. Alex stopped to talk to them. He motioned towards the house—up to her window—and she shrank back against the curtains.

When she looked again his Jeep had disappeared and the men were melting back into the shadows.

Security?

What had she got herself into?

She needed to get out of here. If he thought she was going to sit here calmly and wait for him…

She wouldn't speak to the press. She'd go and find Spiros. She could have fun helping him set up his boatyard.

It'd be more fun than sitting here waiting.

Maybe that was what royal princesses did—sat and waited for their men to have time for them.

Not this one.

CHAPTER TWELVE

By THE time Lily had figured out the car, the baby seat, the logistics of getting the garage roller door raised, she was more than flustered. She was fuming.

It was all very well for Alex to buy her a car and blithely say *go visit your friends if you want*. But he didn't have to juggle strollers, baby bottles, diaper bags and a baby who decided just as she strapped him into the car that he had other plans. Which necessitated taking him out of the car, heading for the bathroom, then figuring out a whole new wardrobe for both of them.

'Though it's just as well we weren't halfway down the coast road,' she told Michales ruefully. 'I want Spiros to be pleased to see me.'

But at last she was ready.

As she swung out into the rhododendron drive, a grey saloon swung in behind her. It stayed about a hundred yards behind, speeding up when she speeded up, slowing when she slowed.

Was this something she had got accustomed to?

'These'll be your father's heavies,' she told Michales. 'Where were they when you needed changing or when I was trying to fold up the stroller?' She glowered into the rear-view mirror. 'If you guys intend to stick with me, your job description's about to change.'

But, inexplicably, her mood was lifting. The morning was gorgeous. The sun was sparkling off the ocean like the diamonds that had given the isles their name. The islands of Khryseis and Argyros looked mysterious and wonderful on the horizon. They were nations now in their own right. When she had a boat she could explore them.

'With my bodyguards chuffing along behind me,' she reminded herself and managed a grin.

Defiant, she slowed, opened the sun roof and hit the sound system. Hey! Alex had set Abba on for her.

He was a very nice man, she decided. And so sexy he made her toes curl. Her very own prince!

She hit 'play' and sang along at the top of her voice, grinning at Michales in the rear-view mirror.

Happy—yet defiant.

That was how she felt. Not a princess, she thought. Just…normal.

So what did Alex think he was doing, supplying her with a luxury car and a couple of bodyguards, then going off to play banker?

Maybe she was being unfair.

This was what Mia and her mother had spent their lives trying to achieve, she thought. Fame. Riches.

Lily's aim of independence came a very poor third.

But I don't want to be independent any more, a small voice whispered in the back of her head.

Just as well, she thought. When she was followed by security men. When she wasn't allowed to talk to the press.

Her vague sense of unease deepened. Was what had happened over the last three days a fantasy?

She slowed as she passed the palace. Somewhere within that vast confection of turrets, towers and general ostentation was Alex. Trying to sort things out.

Without her.

So he still had his independence. While she stayed…where she was supposed to stay.

'I don't want to stay in the palace,' she told Michales but she knew she was lying.

Where you go, I will go, and where you lodge, I will lodge, your people shall be my people…

Ruth had it right, Lily thought. Where her love went, there was her home.

She'd fallen so deeply in love that if Alex needed to live surrounded by chandeliers—or if he needed to live in Manhattan— then that was where she should be, too.

He didn't want her. Not like that.

She couldn't sustain her happiness. The unease was too great. For the last three days she'd allowed herself to believe in happy endings.

Today was the beginning of reality.

Alex pulled up in the castle courtyard. Nikos was waiting. He'd asked his cousin to be here.

'Hey,' Nikos said, strolling across the forecourt to grasp his friend's hand. 'How goes it?'

'Fine,' Alex said. And then he grinned. 'Maybe even great. I'm thinking we have a chance of getting this sorted. Thanks for doing this for me. I didn't want to face these vultures alone.'

'I thought you had Lily here,' Nikos said.

'She's over at the hideaway.'

'She didn't want to be here?'

'This is nothing to do with her.'

'Right,' Nikos said. Then he shook his head. 'Nope. Not right. Aren't you two married?'

'Yeah, but…'

'Then she's supposed to be here.'

'You think Lily will understand one part of what these guys are saying?'

'You think I will?'

'You're here for moral support.'

'Right,' Nikos said again, dryly, contenting himself with a quizzical look without further comment. He took his friend's arm. 'Okay, let's go. But, before we do this, there's something you should see.'

'What?'

'Lily's mother is in Athens. Mia's mother. She's been talking to the press. If you and Lily aren't having problems already, I suspect you're about to now.'

Okay, she wasn't speaking to the press but Alex hadn't forbidden her to shop.

Feeling strange and self-conscious and more than a little nervous, Lily swung the big car into Sappheiros's main shopping square.

She was feeling ever so slightly defiant. She might do something really shocking. Like…like buying sexy lingerie.

There was a thought.

She found herself grinning, shoving the unease aside. Do it, she told herself.

She parked. Her grey shadow parked two cars up, and two grey-suited men climbed out.

She emerged from the car and waved to them. They looked taken aback.

'Can one of you guys unfold my stroller?' she called, hauling it out of the trunk and looking at it as if it were a weapon of mass destruction. How could a stroller be so complicated?

The men hesitated. Clearly they'd been told to stay in the background.

'Are you guys paid to look after me or not?' she demanded, and they looked at each other and finally the oldest shrugged.

'Yes, ma'am.'

'Hooray,' she said, unclipping Michales from his car seat.

'Then we'd appreciate some help. His Highness, Prince Michales, has no transport until his stroller is erected.'

Two minutes later she had Michales in his stroller. She was wandering along the shop fronts.

Everyone was looking at her.

She wasn't half obvious, she thought dryly. Young mum taking baby for a walk, with two beefcakes following about three feet behind.

She stopped. She turned. 'Do you guys ever back off?'

'We're not permitted to let you out of our sight,' one said.

'Fine,' she said and glowered and, before they knew what she was doing, she'd pushed the stroller back to them. 'I'm off to buy a newspaper and then find somewhere to buy a coffee. You can stare at me through the café window if you must. Take care of His Highness.'

She'd meant it as a joke. She was going to buy herself a newspaper and then return to Michales before she bought her coffee.

Only… Only…

Thanks to her father's love of scholarship, she could read Greek. Not well, but enough.

The photograph caught her eye before she'd even purchased the paper. She picked it up numbly.

Grey Suit Two was suddenly beside her, pulling out his wallet. 'We pay,' he said.

'Like hell you do,' she muttered, still staring in horror at the front page. But then she realised she had no choice. She'd had not a moment since she'd arrived on the island to arrange currency conversion. 'Okay. Pay for them all,' she said, motioning to the array of newspapers on the counter. 'I'll pay you back later. And, while you're at it, kindly give me enough money for a coffee. Then leave me alone. Look after Michales and don't come near me.'

And then she thought she sounded like Mia. She winced. Royal arrogance was so not her thing.

'And buy yourselves coffee,' she called after him. 'And something to eat. Whatever you fancy. I'll reimburse you for that, too.'

Feeling a tiny bit better, she found a coffee shop. It looked nice and dark in its recesses—a Diamond Isles version of Ye Olde Nautical Coffee Shoppe. The patrons were shadows. It was so gloomy the girl behind the counter didn't recognise her.

Which was excellent. She was starting to crave anonymity.

She found a seat at the furthermost table and started reading the papers.

And stopped feeling better.

The girl brought her coffee. She swallowed the first mouthful so fast she burnt her mouth.

She had three papers spread out around her now. Their headlines shouted, in sequence:

'My Triumph: Two Royal Daughters.'

And:

'My Clever Lily—Taught to be a Princess From Birth.'

And:

'Alexandros Never Stood A Chance Against My Princess Lily.'

Here it all was, laid out for the world to see. Her mother's naked ambition. Her mother's connivance, her ruthlessness, her fight to get the glory for her daughters that she felt she'd been cheated of herself.

Her mother was the second daughter of the second daughter of a princess. If only she'd been the first son of a first son of a king… She spelled it out. Her anger and humiliation at being raised as second-rate royalty. Her betrayal by her husband, who should have been richer, should have enjoyed the limelight his aristocratic birth entitled him to. Her fight to get Mia to where she should be in the world and her pride that Mia had gone from being Queen to being fabulously rich as well.

And now…and here was the implication…through incredible planning, forethought, cunning, here was Lily, her second daughter, claiming the throne in turn. Not as Queen but Crown Princess. Almost as good as her sister.

This, according to her mother, was the culmination of a family dream. She was travelling now to be with her. Her clever daughter.

Lily felt sick.

The girl came up to collect her coffee cup. She stared at the papers and then she stared more closely at Lily.

'It is,' she breathed.

'It is what?' Lily said dully.

'You're her.' The girl pointed to a picture of Lily, inset on a much larger picture of her mother looking triumphant. 'You're Princess Lily.'

'I'm not a princess.'

'Oh, but you are,' the girl breathed. 'I'd love to be a princess. I read the papers after your wedding. There was a picture of you on the beach with your baby, and I thought you looked lovely. You looked like it could even be a marriage for love.' She sighed theatrically. 'But now your mother tells us how it really is…' She clasped her hands over her heart. 'My Carlos is a fisherman and he's poor, but even if a prince offered, I'd give him up for my Carlos. Your prince has to marry you for honour. I see that. But my Carlos will marry me for love.'

She carried away Lily's empty cup with her moral high ground, and Lily was left feeling even more sick.

She went back to the papers.

There was no condemnation of Alex. Alex was seen as virtuous for having done the right thing under extraordinary circumstances. He was morally fine.

Michales remained heir to the throne. He was okay, too.

But she wasn't. Lily was now being portrayed as another of these women who sold themselves to the highest bidder.

There was resigned acceptance. Alexandros was a good man, the editorials advised. An honourable man. The country was counselled to put their distaste for Lily and her family aside and get on with life.

Outside, Bodyguard One and Bodyguard Two were pacing the pavement with the stroller, taking smaller and smaller circuits of the shopping strip. They were staring in at her with increased hostility.

Had they read the newspapers as well?

This was what they expected of her, she thought dully. That she might abandon Michales, too?

She read on, feeling worse and worse. At the end of the last editorial was a comment, almost an aside:

This newspaper has heard rumours that Prince Alexandros has been asked to take part in a prestigious gardening project in the US. If Alexandros decides to leave any of his royal duties to this woman, we wish to register a very strong protest. Princess Lily has made an extremely advantageous marriage. Let her be content with that. We note the Prince has not brought this woman to the palace. So be it. Let this woman and her objectionable mother stay out of our lives.

And finally… There was a picture of three rings—the caption labelled them the rings of the Diamond Isles. The Sappheiros ring was sapphire with three diamonds. The Argyros ring was silver with three diamonds. The Khryseis ring was gold, again with three diamonds.

Apparently they'd been locked in a bank vault for generations, only for use by the Crown Princess of each country.

They were…exquisite.

The editorial went on:

Let the women who wear these rings be truly deserving of the honour. They've sat in the bank vaults since Giorgos's forebears dissolved the principalities. We note Alexandros did not use the Sappheiros ring on the occasion of his marriage. Now we understand why.

She stared down at the plain gold band on her finger for a long time—then twisted it off and shoved it to the bottom of her jeans pocket.

Her cellphone rang. She answered it absently, still staring at a full face photograph of her mother. Her mother? The woman who smirked up from the photograph didn't deserve the title.

'Lily?'

Alex. Of course it was Alex. She was out in the public eye, disobeying orders. It was a wonder her phone had stayed silent this long.

Let this woman and her objectionable mother stay out of our lives.

'Have you seen the papers?' he demanded.

'I'm reading them now. What "prestigious gardening project"?'

'That's nothing. Your mother…'

'Is being objectionable. Of course. What project?'

'Can you ask her to shut up?'

That was it. No apology. No thought that this might hurt.

'I haven't spoken to my mother for five years.'

'She's still your mother.'

'So she says.'

He got it then. The anger. She heard him register, regroup. Even turn placatory. 'What she said…it doesn't make any dif-ference,' he told her.

'Of course it makes a difference.'

'If she's nothing to do with you…'

'I'm still her daughter. One of her two daughters, both of whom are on the take. Do you think I'll sit back and let your country think that of me?'

'It's nonsense. Lily, they'll see you're different.'

'While you go back and forth to Manhattan and keep on with your very prestigious project. That you haven't talked to me about.'

She heard a sharp intake of breath. Then… 'Lily, I need to organise…'

'Of course you need to organise,' she cut in. 'I don't need an explanation.'

'Lily, what is this? The guys tell me you're sitting in a public café. Can people hear?'

'Of course they can hear,' she said, looking around as she spoke and realising that every person in the café was listening. The waitress had turned off the radio. Her words were being broadcast to an audience.

Whatever she said now would be carried from one end of the island to the other by nightfall, she realised. So be it. If she was intending to be resolute, the time was now.

'I'm on my way to Spiros's boatyard,' she said, speaking distinctly in Greek so every occupant of the café could understand. 'And then I'll talk to the local realtors. I need a house somewhere down by the harbour.'

There was a stunned silence. Then, 'Lily, what are you talking about?'

'My future. As a boat-builder.'

'We'll be living in the palace.'

'You'll be living wherever you want to live, but I want a home for me and Michales. I'm not talking money. A bedsit will do fine. I'm not my mother's daughter, Alex, no matter what the press says.'

'I never said you were.'

'It doesn't matter what you said. It's what the islanders believe. But I'm *not* her daughter.'

She was getting loud. Good. She felt like yelling. She felt like picking up chairs and flinging them through windows.

For the last few days she'd been exploring this wonderful new sensation of having a life. A future. Michales and Alex both.

But marriage to Alex was a fairy tale. She'd been kidding herself. Fairy tales were for children's books. What Alex was planning for her was no fairy tale. Living in the palace as a princess, with the islanders hating her and Alex coming and going as he pleased. Or being left in his hideaway while he did…whatever he wanted to do.

'I've married you so Michales can stay as your legitimate heir, and so you can govern,' she said, feeling cold and sick but knowing she had to say this. 'But that's all. I'm not a princess. I'll live in a house by the harbour. You can have all the access you want to Michales, as long as he comes home to me every night. But the royalty bit is yours. Do whatever you want but don't factor me in. Now, if you'll excuse me, I need to find Spiros. We have a future together. You and I don't.'

Alex had another meeting scheduled, in what…three minutes? Nikos couldn't handle this alone.

He needed to get down to the docks and talk to her.

'She can build her boats while she lives here,' he muttered but he knew this was a deeper problem.

The butler entered, carrying iced water in an exquisite crystal glass on a silver tray. The elderly servant raised his brow in a question, thinking he'd been talking to him.

'Sir?'

Hell, he had to talk to someone. 'The Princess Lily,' he snapped. 'She stays here.'

'Of course,' the man said. 'Will her mother be staying here, too, sir?'

'No!'

'Queen Mia's mother has her own apartment here.'

'Board it up,' Alex snapped. 'It won't be needed. That woman comes here over my dead body.'

'And…the Princess Lily?'

'She's saying the same thing about herself,' he growled. 'Which is a nonsense.'

'The country wouldn't mind if she didn't live here,' the man said diffidently. 'The islanders understand this is a marriage of convenience.'

'That's what she thinks.'

'It's what everybody thinks,' the man said, and then gave a discreet cough and glanced at his watch. 'Your meeting, sir.'

'Damn my meeting.'

'It's the bankers from Switzerland. They hold the titles to…'

'I know damn well what they hold the titles to. Nikos can take over. I need to go…'

'To the docks?' the man said, raising his brow politely again.

'Yes. And I won't need a chauffeur,' he snapped. 'This is between Lily and me.'

'Yes, sir,' the man said woodenly and stood, waiting.

'What are you waiting for?'

'To collect your glass.'

'How much are these glasses worth?' Alex said, in a voice his friends would have recognised as dangerous.

'They're antique,' the man said. 'Priceless.'

'So if I tossed it into the fireplace…'

'You could well create a scandal.'

'Use plastic ones.'

'Pardon?'

'Or, better still, jam jars. I can smash jam jars.'

'I don't know if…'

'Of course you have jam jars,' he snapped. 'You have jam for breakfast, don't you?'

'King Giorgos favoured smoked salmon.'

'Well, here's my first household order as new ruler,' Alex growled, sounding like a man driven. 'I want jam for breakfast. In jars. This might be a palace but it has to be a home as well.'

'Yes, sir.' Not a muscle quivered. 'But, sir, the meeting… I don't believe Nikos can…'

'I don't believe Nikos can either,' he said and sighed and set his glass—carefully—on the silver tray. 'I'll deal with the titles. It'll take hours but they have to be sorted. But Lily straight after.'

'Yes, sir. I'll tell them you're ready.' He walked out of the room in stately style—but paused at the entrance. 'And the Princess Lily's mother? She's contacted the staff to say she'll be here on the afternoon ferry. Did you…er…mean it about your dead body?'

'I guess not.'

But then he hesitated. Something told him he needed to get this right. Lily's mother. He thought for a minute. He thought of what this woman had done. Lily's mother? Did she deserve the title?

'Or maybe…yes,' he said slowly. 'Maybe I did mean it. Where is it that Mia's living now?'

'I believe she's still in Dubai.'

'Dubai.' He grimaced. 'Damn, I don't have time…'

The man coughed. Discreetly. This discretion was like another language.

Maybe he ought to listen.

'Yes?' he said.

'If I may venture a suggestion, sir,' the butler said. 'If you're under pressure… There are some things you can't delegate but you have a full staff here waiting to serve you. Until now you've used us reluctantly. But…' he met Alex's gaze square on '…but it would be a privilege for us to actually serve you.'

Alex stared at him, bemused.

A full staff…waiting to work for him.

He was royal.

It would be a privilege for us to actually serve you.

He hadn't figured it until now. Until right now.

It cut both ways.

'I have a palace secretary,' he said slowly.

'Yes, sir.'

'Giorgos's man?'

'I believe he would wish to serve *you*,' the man said, still discreet but his message was crystal clear. 'As you wish to serve the islanders.'

'And the Princess Lily?'

'If she's truly to be your wife, then that service would, of course, extend to her.'

'Then send him in,' Alex said slowly. 'Tell the Swiss guys I'll be with them in ten minutes… Give them something stronger than water in those ridiculous glasses—and yes, I'll need a fast car and a chauffeur as soon as the meeting finishes. But dammit,' he added, 'I meant what I said about the jam.'

The man's wooden countenance cracked, just a little. He allowed himself an infinitesimal echo of a smile.

'Yes, Your Highness. Certainly, Your Highness,' he said and left, closing the door carefully after him.

It took five hours.

Five hours spent beginning to sort out the mess that was the island's financial affairs might not seem long, but they were the longest hours Alex could remember. But finally he was free. Finally he could drive down to the harbour. Or be driven. Fast. By a driver who looked as if things were finally slotting into the natural order.

But Alex didn't have time to think about order. He strode into Spiros's boatshed and stared in astonishment.

Lily was underneath a boat.

He'd had this place set up for Spiros. It was a great little shed, right on the main Sappheiros harbour. Last time he'd seen it, it had been empty, waiting for its new tenant.

Now it contained six men, two women and one baby. They were clustered around what he recognised as his boat. He could see where it had been towed in—sand and bits of rotten timber had trailed in its wake.

How on earth had she got it here so fast?

Lily was at work already. She'd wriggled under the bow of the dinghy and was prodding each plank in turn, while everyone else watched from the sides.

'It's a great project to start with,' she was saying to Spiros. 'This'll keep us happy until we get the materials to start bigger projects.'

'Lily.'

She hadn't seen him enter. He saw her freeze at the sound of his voice. Her expression became almost defiant—and then she went back to what she was doing.

'We can restore it exactly as it was,' she said, only the faintest of tremors acknowledging his presence. 'See these joins? See how they slot together? That's real craftsmanship. The guys who built this really knew their stuff. I need to do some research before we start.'

'We have an Internet connection at the palace,' Alex said loudly into the silence.

'That's right,' she responded, as if he were just another voice from the outside. 'I'll need an Internet connection at my house.' She was being as businesslike with him as she was with Spiros.

'You won't need anything at your house. We need to live at the palace.'

He was ignored. 'My laptop's a bit old but it should be okay. Can we get broadband at the harbour?'

'I said we'll live at the palace.'

Finally she acknowledged him. She hauled herself out from under the boat, pulled herself upright and dusted herself off.

'No,' she said simply, 'I'll not live at the palace.'

'Why not?'

'My mother's living at the palace. Haven't you seen the papers?'

He shook his head. 'She won't be.'

'She said…'

'No matter what she said.'

This conversation should be private, but first he had to break through this icy indifference. 'There's a generous lifetime allowance allocated to Mia as Giorgos's widow,' he told her. He told them all. 'I'm the administrator. This morning I converted part of it into a permanent travel fund for your mother. She's been handed first class air tickets to Dubai, and hotel vouchers. The travel allowance will be ongoing. Wherever Mia moves, the funds will pay for flights and luxurious accommodation so your mother and Mia can stay together for ever.'

There was a deathly hush. The onlookers didn't understand.

Lily understood. Her anger faltered. She gazed at him in awe. And…magically, the beginning of laughter.

'They'll kill each other,' she whispered at last.

'Excellent.' He ventured a smile.

Which was maybe a mistake. 'Don't you dare smile at me,' she snapped. She was obviously trying to haul herself together. Remembering where she was—remembering her grievances. 'What you've done for my mother…it's all very well, but if you think you can buy me…'

'I never thought I could buy you.'

'You're going to Manhattan. While I stay in the palace? No way.'

'We need to talk about that.'

'We don't,' she said crossly.

'I have to talk to you.'

'So who's going to make me?' she said softly.

There was a stifled laugh from the onlookers. This was an impossible conversation to have in public.

'Please, Lily. I need to talk to you alone.'

'I'm busy.'

'Mending *my* boat.'

'Don't you want it mended?'

'Yes, but…'

'There you go then. Can we send you the account? Spiros, this can be our first local commission.'

'Lily!'

'Yes…Your Highness?' she said, raising her brows in mute enquiry. 'Was there anything else you wanted?'

'I want you!'

'I don't see why.'

She turned her back on him, talking to Spiros. 'Let's write up a list of materials we need,' she said. 'You want to do it in your office? Eleni, can you take care of Michales for a few more minutes? If you'll excuse us…'

He moved, barring her way. She was back in her bib-and-brace overalls and her baseball cap. Did she have any idea how cute she looked? Did she have any idea how desperate she made him feel? Or how inadequate. 'Lily, I need to talk to you. Now!'

'Maybe you'd better listen,' Eleni said uneasily. 'His Highness has been very good to us.'

'To you. Maybe not to me.'

'He brought you to this place,' Eleni said. 'He's making you a princess.'

'I don't want to be a princess.'

'Every girl wants to be a princess,' Eleni said.

'Would you want to be a princess?' Lily demanded, rounding on Eleni. 'If it meant not being married to Spiros.'

Eleni gazed at her in confusion. 'Spiros is…different.'

'How different?'

'He's Spiros,' she said, looking at her rotund and balding husband with affection. 'He loves me,' Eleni said. 'This isn't a fair comparison.'

'It's not, is it,' Lily agreed. She turned back to Alex. 'See?

Spiros loves Eleni. There's no negotiation there. They went to America together. They came here together.'

'You're saying you want to go to Manhattan?'

She shook her head, looking angry. 'You don't want me in that part of your life,' she said flatly. 'And the islanders don't want me in their face either. But it's okay. The realtor's been here and he's shown me the perfect house. Two bedrooms, so Michales and I don't have to share unless we want, and it over-looks the harbour. We'll live happily ever after. Now, if we could get on…'

'Lily, talk to me,' he said through gritted teeth, and Eleni grinned and gave Lily a push in the small of her back.

'Go with him before he explodes,' she advised. 'He's very close to exploding. I can see this.'

'It doesn't matter if he does explode.'

'It'd make a mess,' Eleni retorted. 'As did hauling in this boat. Why you had to tell Spiros about it today… You knew he wouldn't rest until he had it. So off you go, the pair of you. Spiros,' she said sharply, 'help me.'

And suddenly Spiros was behind Alex, Eleni was behind Lily and they were being propelled out of the boatshed. They were outside before they had a chance to argue, and the boat-shed doors were slammed shut behind them.

So they were suddenly out on the docks. The berths were all empty. A lone seagull was preening itself on a bollard. Water lapped against the pilings.

There was no one in sight.

'Where…where are all the fishing boats?' Lily asked, sounding desperate, looking desperate.

'Out fishing. Lily, you can't do this.'

'I can,' she said gamely. 'I will. My house is over there.' She pointed across the harbour. 'It's the one with window boxes. It's not only you who'll have a garden.'

'Do you really want to live alone?'

'With Michales. But yes.'

'Why?'

'Because I'm not about to follow my mother's and my sister's example. I hadn't realised it until I saw the newspapers—how much damage they did. But do you think I can stay around as your wife now?'

'Of course you can.'

'When you're not here?'

He was trying his hardest to figure this out.

He'd thought he had it figured on the way here. He did have it sorted. He loved this woman. They could do this. But the explanations he'd prepared seemed to have disappeared into confusion.

'I will need to leave you sometimes,' he said slowly. He wasn't about to lie to her now. 'If you have your boat-building… I need something. I can't only be a prince.'

'That's just it,' she said, indignation fading. 'I have no right to expect anything. It's a token marriage.'

He shook his head. 'How can it be a token marriage when we share a bed? When you've asked me to be faithful and I've taken the same promise from you?'

'I shouldn't have done either. Alex, please, I've been out of control for too long. What I want is to get my life together. I had this notion back at your lovely house that I could sink into your life—make it my own. Only, of course, that's dumb. I don't want the people of the Diamond Isles looking at me the same way they look at Mia and my mother. I have to carve my own way.'

'And I fit in where?'

'Nowhere,' she said forlornly. 'Not as your wife. I've been trying to figure it out and I can't see it. For you to be a part-time prince and leave me as a full-time princess…'

'You do want me to stay here all the time?'

'I don't want you to do anything.' She was close to tears. 'I have no right to want anything of you, other than support for Michales. I need nothing.'

'You deserve everything.'

'I have everything,' she said, flatly but surely. She tilted her face so the sun shone full on it. 'I have my son. I have my life. I have a career I love, in one of the most beautiful settings in the world. What more can I ask for?'

'Me.' It was an egotistical answer—maybe dumb—but it was what he needed to say. He wanted her to want him.

He wanted this woman.

But she was shaking her head. 'I daren't ask that,' she whispered. 'Because if I let myself ask…'

'I might just give?'

'Would you?' she asked. 'How much would you give?'

He was struggling here, trying to work out where she was going. Trying to understand. This morning he'd woken up beside her and the world had been at his feet. But now…

He'd pushed it too hard. He knew he had. But how to get it back?

She looked…scared, he thought. Angry and defiant but, deep down, terrified.

Should he back off?

How could he back off? What would happen if their marriage was simply in name only?

He'd be gutted.

A marriage of convenience…

What the hell was he doing?

A memory came back, piercing into his conscience from a time he'd tried desperately to block. His mother, lying on a bed of pillows on one of the ledges jutting out from a rock path leading to the sea. She'd been back on the island for such a short time before she'd become ill. They'd planned their garden together, and he was building it. It was all he could do for her.

He'd been planting the rock wall with scented geraniums.

She'd called down to him. He'd looked up, his hands covered with loam—filthy, happy, the sun on his face, where he most wanted to be in the world.

'Mama?'

'I love you,' she'd said, so softly he hardly heard. 'No, don't stop what you're doing. It's just…I thought it and I needed to tell you… It's the only important thing and you need to remember it. I love you.'

Two months later she was dead, and somehow the message she'd given him had been…not forgotten exactly, for it had helped mould who he was. But he hadn't thought of that love as extending from what he and his mother had shared.

Only of course it had extended. As love must.

Loving. He had it, right here, in this woman before him— his Lily, looking at him now, troubled, battered by her mother's betrayal, confused and hurt by what he'd done this morning but, even in her confusion, looking to the future. Trying to make the best of what he'd given her.

This woman was his wife. What was he doing, messing with it?

Start with Lily, he told himself, feeling dazed.

'Alex, what is it?'

'I wasn't going to Manhattan to work on a project,' he told her. 'I never was.'

'You were going…'

'To wind up the company. To put it into the hands of a couple of competent employees, and to offer to keep a role as offshore consultant. I thought I might be able to go over occasionally…but not often.'

'There's no need…'

'There is a need,' he said softly. 'I should have told you. And I should have asked you, too. Lily, will you marry me?'

Marry…

He obviously wasn't making sense. She stood in the afternoon sun and she stared at him as if he were speaking an unknown language.

Maybe he was.

'I've already married you,' she whispered.

'Yes, but it wasn't right.'

'I don't know what you mean.'

'I think you do.' He caught her hands and held. 'It wasn't true. This time I want to stand before a priest I know and love, beside a woman I know and love, and I want to make my vows and keep them.'

'But…why…?'

'Your illness…'

'No,' she snapped and the sudden flare of hope in her face disappeared to nothing. 'Don't you dare feel sorry for me.'

She tried to drag her hands away but he wasn't releasing them.

'No, Lily, wait. I'm not saying this because I feel sorry for you. How can I feel sorry when I'm so proud I'm close to bursting with pride? That a woman like you would stoop to marry me… Lily, we did this the wrong way round. I married you as a royal bride. I stood before the islanders and said you were my wife. And then I took you home to a place which can't be our home. It's a place where we can stay hidden, it's a place for time out, but now's not the time for hiding.'

'But I don't want…'

'You don't want to be a princess by yourself,' he said, still sure that he was right. 'But what if you weren't by yourself? What if you were half of a whole…half of the ruling royal couple of Sappheiros…?'

'The islanders would never agree.'

'They never will if you stay hidden. Lily, I'm asking you again. I want to marry you, but this time I want it to be between us. I want to declare my love for you. And then I want to start making reparation for both of us.'

'Both…'

'We've been robbed,' he said slowly. 'It's taken me a while to see it but now I do. Royalty robbed me of my childhood. My mother had to leave me behind and I've blamed more than Giorgos for that loss. I blamed this role. I blamed royalty. I wanted desperately to help the islanders, to rule so I could set things right, but I didn't want to commit myself. That's how I married you.'

'So what's changed now?'

'You,' he said softly and tugged her in so her breasts rested against his chest. 'I nearly had it. I thought this morning that I'd head to Manhattan and close things up there, then come back and see what I could do. Only I should have told you, asked you to come with me. I had a hell of a day with financiers and that was daft, too. You know why? Because I had Nikos there, trying desperately to be a friend, to understand. Only he has problems of his own on Argyros. You know who should have been there? You.'

'You think I could understand financiers?' She was bewildered, he thought. He wasn't explaining this right.

'No,' he said lovingly. 'No one could understand that lot. I've set my lawyers onto them. But they had to talk to me first and I came away hornswoggled…'

'Hornswoggled…'

'Hornswoggled,' he repeated. 'Great word. Pity it's not Greek. But I wanted to be hornswoggled with you, and the only person I had was Nikos—and he was busy telling me I'd done everything wrong. But, Lily, I'm losing track here. I love you. Will you marry me?'

He was holding her at arm's length so he could watch her face. He was watching her confusion. He was aching for it to disappear.

'I guess I don't have to ask you to marry me,' he conceded. 'Not officially, for you've already done that. But what I want now… I want more. I want you to trust me.'

She nodded. The confusion was fading. She was as serious as he was. 'That's a very different thing.'

'So?'

'I think I already do trust you,' she whispered but he shook his head.

'You don't trust me to care for you. You don't trust me to be beside you, whatever life throws at either of us. You've been alone all your life. You expect more of the same. You say you want to live down at the harbour. Do you really want to live on your own?'

'No, but…'

'But if you live with me, you'll be fearful that it'll be on my terms.'

'That's reasonable. You don't want…'

'It's not reasonable,' he said. 'I've just figured it out. I want you to live with me, but on your terms.'

'Alex, you're a prince.'

'I am a prince,' he said softly. 'But what does that mean? I need to earn the respect of my people, as I need to gain your respect and trust. Can I start with you and work my way out? Can we marry for real?

'For we're not properly married,' he said. 'You didn't walk down the aisle with Spiros to give you away. We didn't get married in front of Father Antonio. And we didn't go straight to the palace and stand on the balcony and wave and kiss each other in front of the whole island and I didn't say to the world I'm so proud of you that if anything, anyone, even implies that you're not totally perfect I'll have them tossed into a good deep dungeon for high treason.'

'A dungeon,' she said faintly. 'Do we have dungeons?'

'I'll have them dug on the off chance,' he said grandly. 'Lily, what do you say?'

'I…'

'I love you, Lily,' he said hurriedly, before she had a chance to answer. 'This is the most important moment in my life. I stared at those newspaper headlines this morning and I thought that if I were you I'd walk away and never come back. And I wouldn't blame you. I might have known you'd do the noble thing instead. Move out, stay married, take the flak but get on with your own life as best you could. Lily, please, could you include me?'

'Um…okay,' she ventured and he held her back at arm's length so he could look into her eyes.

'Just okay?'

'Okay, Your Majesty?' she tried.

'Not…okay, my love?'

'You want me to be a princess.'

'Not *a* princess. *My* princess.'

'You'll be my prince.'

'That's the idea.'

'Does that mean I have to take off my dungarees?'

'For the wedding, maybe, but afterwards… I see us as the people's prince and princess,' he said and he pulled her against him and was holding her so their hearts were suddenly beating in synch. She could feel it. Magic.

Magic!

Move over, Cinderella, she thought. This prince is mine!

'So where does that leave us?' she whispered.

'It leaves us planning our future,' he said, awed by the vision. 'In between government duties I'll design gardens from one end of this island to the other. When I finish here I'll start on the gardens of Argyros and Khryseis. And, as for you… The fishing fleet on the three islands is in shocking condition. Shocking!'

'Really?' she whispered, starting to smile.

'You'll be appalled when you see. I think you have a job for life.'

'I love you,' she said.

'You do?'

'I do.'

'Will you say that in front of Father Antonio?'

'I'll say that in front of the world if you want me to.'

'So you'll marry me? Properly? With your heart?'

There was only one answer to that. 'When?'

'How about now? If I can get Father Antonio away from his fishing, if there's no funeral and if he has a clean cassock… Why not now?'

'Just…just us?'

'And Nikos to hold me up,' he said promptly. 'He'll never forgive me otherwise. Stefanos is in New York, but we're not waiting that long.'

'We need a photographer,' she whispered, her eyes alive with laughter. And something else. A joy so great he could see it.

'Why would we want a photographer?'

'Because this is a real wedding,' she said and, astonishingly, she was starting to sound efficient. 'I need photographs to show our grandchildren.' Then she paused—and blushed. 'I mean…eventually Michales might have children. I might even be a grandma. I might…'

And he watched her eyes widen as the implication of what they were about to do sank in.

He laughed. He felt as if the weight of the world had shifted from his shoulders.

They could do this. Together they could face their future and plan and laugh and love.

'What if we let the two reporters who met us on the beach know what's happening?' he suggested. 'A scoop.'

'Wow,' Lily said and she was smiling. A chameleon smile— from anger to laughter in seconds. 'Okay. Deal. Can I tell Spiros and Eleni? They'll have to come.'

'I suspect they've guessed,' he said wryly and glanced at the boatshed door—which closed very quickly. 'Spiros will give you away? What about in three hours? Seven o'clock. Right on sunset. The photographs will be fabulous, for us or for our grandchildren. If I can find Father Antonio.'

Her smile didn't fade. 'You'll have to do the organisation,' she warned. 'I have sawdust under my fingernails. A girl has some pride. You go find the priest and I'll go let Eleni turn me into a bride.'

'Lily…'

'Mmm?'

He kissed her gently on the lips. Tenderly. Then he set her back from him again. There was still something he needed to say. 'Lily, I want the islanders to know the truth about you.'

'The truth…'

'I will not let them go one minute more than I must, thinking you abandoned your son. Please…will you trust me to tell them?'

'I don't like…'

'I know you don't like,' he said. 'But the time for protecting your mother and your sister is past. We need to move forward and the only way we can do this is with truth. Do you trust me to tell your story?'

He was looking at her with such gravitas… Her Alexandros.

'I trust you with my heart,' she whispered. 'With my life.'

'It's the greatest gift a man can be given,' he said and pressed her hand to his heart. 'And I'll honour it as long as I breathe.'

CHAPTER THIRTEEN

ALEX left.

The door of the boatshed opened.

Maybe she had to move. Maybe she had to speak.

'Eleni?' she ventured but the word came out a squeak.

Eleni was the closest thing to a mother Lily knew. Alex had brought Spiros and his family here as part of her future. These people were her future.

She couldn't do this without them.

'What is it?' Eleni demanded, looking torn between awe and fear. 'Lily, what's happened? You haven't sent him away?'

'Just for a bit,' Lily confessed. 'Until seven.'

'What's happening at seven?'

'That's something I thought I might talk to you about,' she said, suddenly feeling absurd. Dumb. Crazy.

'What?'

She walked back into the boatshed. She had the attention of everyone, including the men who worked for Spiros.

'I thought I might get married,' she said, and the silence was deafening. 'Sort of like last time,' she added, sounding defensive. 'Only different. Only...' She gasped and could hardly go on. 'Only for ever.'

More silence. More and more silence.

And then… 'At seven,' Eleni said at last, and this time it was Eleni's voice that came out a high-pitched squeak.

'I need a dress,' Lily told her.

'The one you wore last time?' Eleni said.

'That was everybody's dress. The royal bridal gown. I want my own.'

'In three hours.' Eleni was squealing for real now. 'In three… Look at you!'

'Don't I look like a bride?'

'You're making fun, no?'

'No,' she said, and got serious. 'This is for real. But I want you all there.'

Another long silence. Then, 'Spiros,' Eleni said, rounding on her husband. 'Take a bath.'

'Whaa…?'

'Take a bath,' she ordered. 'Now. It'll take until seven to get the grease off you. You can sit right up the back and…'

'I want Spiros to give me away.'

There was another of those deathly hushes. She was getting used to them.

She looked round at their faces—at their open mouths—and she giggled.

It was either giggle or faint, she thought. She was hysterical, either way.

'Can we do it?' she asked Eleni, and Eleni stared at her for another full, long minute. Lily could practically see lists being written. And then she nodded.

'Yes,' she said at last. 'Shops first. A dress. A dress so fast. Ooh, I want to see the faces of the shopkeepers.'

'They don't like me,' she said.

'You're a princess. They'll love you. They don't know you, is all. Spiros, bath. Boys, get into town. I want flowers. Soft and romantic—tell the florist what it's for and she'll break an arm to get it right. Bouquet for Lily, sprays for me, and single

roses for the men…' Eleni was already on item three on her list
and working down.

This wedding was going to happen.

Nikos was still at the castle. He was deep in a pile of paper-
work, looking put upon.

'I'd rather be fishing,' he said soulfully as Alex entered.
'This ruling business has knobs on it.'

'You need a break,' Alex said. 'How about a wedding?'

Nikos had been entering figures in a ledger. His hand paused
mid-pen-stroke. He turned and looked at his friend, long and
hard. 'Have you been out in the sun?' he asked slowly.

'No,' Alex said and then he grinned. 'Actually, come to think
of it, I have.'

'So whose wedding?'

'Mine.'

'I thought we just did yours.'

'This is sort of a rerun. We're doing it properly this time.'

'I…see,' Nikos said, nodding to hide any confusion he just
might be feeling. 'So…you're thinking of marrying…Lily?'

'How can you doubt it?'

'When?'

Alex glanced at his watch. 'In two hours,' he said. 'Sorry it's
short notice. Father Antonio was fishing!'

Nikos nodded. Bemused. 'He likes to fish, does our Father.
So… You've interrupted him to marry you?'

'That's right.'

'What a truly excellent way to avoid these figures,' Nikos
said and grinned and threw his pen aside. 'A wedding, you say.
Okay, my Prince. Lead the way.'

The leading reporter for the *Sappheiros Times* was halfway
through an article on the Princess Lily's astounding outburst in
a local café when the call came in.

'It's the palace,' the receptionist mouthed to him.

The man sighed. He'd been one of the two men on the beach on Alex's wedding night. His instinct then had been to warm to Lily, but the reports coming in were damning. Her mother's outburst and then Lily's declaration that this was a marriage of convenience were going to cause problems that might even unseat royalty.

The palace secretary would be ringing to attempt to put a different spin on it, he thought. He was accustomed to being bullied by palace officials. Giorgos's threats had made this newspaper almost puppet media.

So what was new?

He picked up the phone with distaste. 'Yes?'

'This is Prince Alexandros. If you can be at the palace in fifteen minutes I have a story for you. A very long story. How soon can you get the presses rolling?'

He didn't like rushed weddings but this…this was different.

Father Antonio glanced into the mirror and thanked God his cassock was clean. There were probably fish scales on his boots, but at least they were covered. He gave his cassock a last twitch, then stepped out into the church proper.

Prince Alexandros was waiting. To his astonishment, Alex was dressed almost casually for a prince, in a simple dark suit, crisp white linen and a tie with boats on.

He'd last seen Alex a little less than two hours ago when he'd hailed him from a friend's boat. He'd been dressed in jeans— this was the Alex that the old priest had known from childhood.

The Alex who smiled at him now was the same. He's a prince no matter what he wears, the old priest thought emotionally. This is as he's always been. He's a man with a good heart.

Nikos, too. He had high hopes for these islands with men like these as rulers.

He looked out over the church. His congregation was tiny.

One Greek lady he knew already—Eleni, cradling a sleeping Michales. They were in the front pew.

In the second pew were the lads from Spiros's boatyard. They looked scrubbed and uncomfortable in their hastily hired suits. They looked as if they'd never worn a suit before.

These boys needed to be introduced to his church, Antonio decided, thinking already which nice girls he could introduce them to.

And then he forgot them. Sophie Krykos had interrupted her evening by the television to play, and play she did. The organ blared out the wedding march.

And at the church door…Spiros and Lily.

Lily's dress was simple. Maybe it was not fit for a princess, the priest thought, but then what did he know of princesses? His job here was to marry this man to this woman and, simple or not, this dress made a man sigh with pleasure.

If he'd been privy to the hysteria in a local dress shop over the last three hours maybe he'd have chuckled but there was no sign of that chaos now. The dress clung to Lily's slight frame as if it had been sewn on her—as, actually, it had been. It was a shimmering lace confection, held by butterfly straps, the bodice arching softly over each breast, clinging to her waist and then flowing outward to form soft folds falling to the floor.

She wore no veil. There were tiny rosebuds threaded into her short-cropped curls. She carried a trailing bouquet of roses and ferns.

She was beautiful.

The priest watched Alex's face and felt his heart swell within him.

He did love a good wedding. A wedding where love was all that mattered. And the look on Alex's face right now…

Love was all that mattered, he thought. Everything else would fall into place.

* * *

She was about to be married. For real.

'Ready?' Spiros asked, patting her arm.

Her prince was at the end of the aisle, waiting to marry her. But it was Alex…simply Alex.

Spiros was nervous. Beads of sweat were building on the boat-builder's brow.

They couldn't both be whimpering heaps. A girl had to have courage. But who needed courage when this was just Alex? Her Alex.

The man she loved with all her heart.

She took his hand and steadied. 'I'm ready, Spiros.'

'Than let's see you married,' Spiros whispered. 'Before I collapse in fright.'

'You don't need to be afraid,' she said. 'It's as Eleni said. When you marry for love it's different. It's as it should be. It's as it is.'

She was a bride in a million. His Lily.

Home was where Lily was, he thought with a flash of insight and he found himself smiling. That she'd agreed to this…

'You still need to go to Manhattan?' Nikos whispered.

He couldn't drag his eyes from Lily. How could she be so beautiful?

'What?'

'Your business,' Nikos teased. 'Is it so important?'

'I can't even remember what it is.'

'Funny about that,' Nikos said, watching Lily start the slow walk up the aisle. 'I believe you're not alone in falling for Lily. I think there's not a man or woman in this church who wouldn't die protecting her. And I suspect the islanders are about to follow.'

But Alex was no longer listening. He was watching his bride walk steadily towards him and he had eyes for no other.

Nikos smiled, fingered the ring in his pocket and decided okay, enough of the talking, he needed to turn into a best man.

* * *

With this ring I thee wed. With my body, I thee worship. All my worldly goods, with thee I share.

She blinked at that. Alex, giving her half his wealth?

This was hardly the time to argue. The priest was waiting for her to repeat the words, as Alex had just repeated them. She'd have to let the wealth thing go.

Now she'd have to let everything go, for Alex was smiling down into her eyes, sliding a ring on her finger, holding her hand for longer than he needed to.

There was that teasing smile. Half laughing but half serious.

The ring… It was the Sappheiros royal ring. A sapphire surrounded by three exquisite diamonds—breathtakingly beautiful.

It was on her finger.

It seemed she was a princess.

As long as we both shall live…

CHAPTER FOURTEEN

ALEX had told one reporter.

He hadn't expected him to share, but share he had. He emerged from the church with his bride on his arm and was confronted by a crush of media.

'Thanks for the heads up,' the reporter he'd talked to called. 'I got the release out. The papers are already on the streets.'

Thus there were even reporters here from Athens. Television crews. Palace staff were appearing, slipping into the crowd. Islanders from all over. Their private ceremony was being gate-crashed.

So be it, he thought. He'd give an even bigger party some time in the not so distant future, when everyone who wanted to be here would be here, when they did the full royal bit and declared Lily to be Crown Princess.

There had to be some really dignified ceremony for that, he thought, and if there wasn't then he'd make one up.

Actually…he hadn't been crowned Crown Prince yet. That meant a double ceremony. A ceremony to share. A life to share. But first…

'We need to go to the palace balcony,' he told his bride. 'We're doing this properly or not at all.'

'It's too late for not at all,' she said, smiling and smiling. 'So I guess the balcony it is.'

It took them half an hour to get back to the palace. The whole island was out to see what was happening. Their chauffeur drove them but they had to drive slowly through the crush.

A woman taking photographs through the car window had a newspaper tucked visibly in her bag. Alex put a hand through the window and snaffled it.

'May I borrow this, ma'am?'

'Keep it,' she called. 'It's my wedding present. Why didn't you tell us about Princess Lily?'

And there it was, emblazoned on the front page.

'Our Princess's Secret.'

Lily all but snatched the paper from his hands. He watched as she read—he watched her face change.

From joy to bewilderment.

'This…this is my story.'

'It is,' he said gently and he wondered if he'd done it wrong.

'I need the islanders to know who you are,' he said gently. 'I can't bear our people not knowing how wonderful you are. I love you and I need our people to love you, too.'

'They'll feel sorry for me,' she whispered, scanning the story he'd told the reporter.

'Maybe for a while,' he said. 'But then they'll be as proud as I am. They'll know they have a princess in a million.'

'Alex…' Her face twisted in distress.

'It's a price,' he said to her softly, holding her close. 'A responsibility. It's why I wanted to keep you at our hideaway a bit longer. But events took us over. Maybe it would be better if the way your mother and sister treated you was never known. But their actions tainted us, and they'll continue to taint us until the truth comes out. I love you, Lily. I'll spend my life protecting you, but we can't hide lies.'

'It's that important?'

'I believe it is. We're going into this marriage proudly,' he said. 'We'll rule this island with pride. With love. With honour.'

'Properly or not at all?' she whispered.

'That's the one.'

'Then I guess properly it is,' she said and she kissed him. And he kissed her.

To the roar of the crowd, he kissed her all the way to the palace.

Then, to the applause of the palace staff, they ran, hand in hand, up the great staircase to the main balcony overlooking the forecourt.

'Can you do this?' Alex asked her, holding her tight.

'Just hold me,' she whispered. 'Hold me for ever. If you hold me, I can do anything.'

Palace protocol was that the Prince kiss his Princess.

Protocol be damned. She kissed him first. And then it was a moot point as to who was kissing who.

Sappheiros had its new royal family.

What followed was a year of wonder…

On the morning of their first anniversary, Lily woke to laughter. They were at the hideaway. Michales was an early riser, but so was Alex. Father and son were out on the balcony, watching the finches in the vines, watching the sea, chuckling at inane manly jokes. The standard hadn't risen past the sausage joke, she thought sleepily. How a girl could love the pair of them was a wonder in itself.

What a year. How could she ever have imagined it would be so good?

This life they'd chosen was unimaginably wonderful. They spent most of their time at the palace, but the palace had changed. Was still changing.

The island had had practically no public buildings. Thus some of the vast palace was now set aside as a truly magnificent library. Meeting rooms. Mothers' clubs, patchwork, anglers' clubs…whatever the islanders needed. The gardens had been made public. The island had been desperate for a new hospital so the palace summer house overlooking the sea was now its base.

She and Alex had worked together to make these things happen. They were a team. His enthusiasm fed hers and vice versa. They lay in bed late at night and made plans. And made love.

There was still a section of the palace retained by them, for their exclusive use. They'd made it a wee bit more of a home. They'd removed a score of chandeliers. They'd introduced jam for breakfast. They'd accepted that it needed to be their permanent home.

For the islanders had taken their royal couple to their hearts. They loved them living in the palace. Finally, they had a real royal family. They had continuity and pride.

She'd accompanied Alex to Manhattan twice now. But Alex drew his plans here, he asked for soil samples to be analysed and the results sent here, he worked on the Internet and constructed plant lists here.

Sappheiros was his home.

As Sappheiros was her home. Lily worked on her boats as Eleni and Spiros played grandparents. Their boatyard was going from strength to strength.

So… She and Alex had their separate careers, but whatever they did, they did where they could come together at nightfall. Where they could stay together as a family.

Family was the best thing, and the times they could escape to the hideaway were delicious.

She was languorously drowsy. Deeply content. Tonight they'd have dinner here, on the balcony, to celebrate their first year of marriage. Alex had wanted to do something special but special was here. And a restaurant with spicy food…maybe not.

'Are you staying in bed till noon?' Alex was standing in the doorway, smiling in at her. He set Michales down and the little boy toddled over to his mother. She tugged him into bed and he crowed with delight.

'We have a gift for you,' Alex said. 'Michales and I. Only you have to get out of bed for us to give it to you.'

'Bed,' Michales said and beamed.

'Can I dress first?'

'Nope,' Alex said. 'Okay, you can put on a wrap. And sandals. That's all. We're too impatient.'

She was intrigued.

He'd been doing something. Part of the cliff between here and the beach had been blocked off for the past year. 'We're worried it's eroding,' Alex had told her, but he'd been here too often for a simple erosion problem.

Something was brewing, she knew. He'd looked mysterious when she'd probed, but definite that she should not go down there.

'Let's go now,' he said and held out an imperious hand. Then, as she didn't move, he strolled over to the bed, bent and kissed her. Deeply. Strongly. Thoroughly. Then he took her hand and tugged her to her feet.

'Come,' he said in his best born-to-rule voice and she giggled and grabbed her wrap and came.

Sure enough, the path that had been cordoned off was now un-cordoned. It led to another cove, just around the cliff from the bay where they swam.

She'd been down this path once when they'd just married but it had been cordoned off straight after.

And now…

She could see why.

This was a garden. Only…what a garden.

It was a waterfall, rock, rough and tumbled, as if tossed together by nature. As she reached the first set of steps, Alex flicked a switch set in the rock—and the waterfall came alive. Water tumbled from above, cascading over rock formations so wonderfully natural she'd have sworn they'd been placed by the gods themselves.

'You made this,' she gasped.

'The water's pumped from the bay with solar power,' he said in quiet satisfaction. 'The sun comes out, the waterfall runs. Water comes from the bay and goes back to the bay.'

She choked with wonder.

'It's my anniversary gift,' he said and held his hand out again. 'Come on. There's more to show you at the bottom.'

The cove at the base of the waterfall was tiny—a miniature version of the cove where they swam. It was a natural harbour formed by two outreaches of cliff. The waterfall ended as a rippling creek that ran beside an ancient boathouse, then over the sand and out to sea.

She'd seen this boathouse twelve months before. It had been dilapidated—about to fall down.

It wasn't dilapidated now. It was gleaming with new paint, pale blue and crisp white, bright and welcoming in its ocean setting. A tiny jetty reached out from the boat doors. Alex's newly restored dinghy was tied at the jetty. The setting was… exquisite.

'Our own boathouse,' Lily breathed. 'Oh…'

'There's more,' Alex said in satisfaction and handed her a key tied with a big blue bow. 'It's from Michales and me. See the soggy end of the bow? It's been sucked personally by the Prince Michales. It should have a royal insignia, but we ran out of time.'

She gazed at her two boys in wonder—her men—and she unlocked the doors.

And drew in her breath.

'Happy anniversary to us,' a sign said inside the door. The banner hung the full length of the boathouse.

And behind it… There was a pile of wood, as wide as it was high. Dressed timber. Tons of it. Enough wood to build…

A boat?

She walked forward, scarcely able to breathe. She touched the nearest plank.

'You haven't,' she breathed.

'I'd like to say I personally dived for it,' Alex said modestly. 'But I'm lousy with a snorkel. I figured you'd want me alive to hold hammers and stuff.'

'It's Huon Pine,' she gasped. 'It's… Alex, there's enough here to build…'

'A yacht?' he asked, hopeful. 'Would you like to build one?'

She was running her fingers from plank to plank, her mind already seeing what she'd build. Twenty-five feet… She stood back. No, thirty. A half cabin. Oh, she'd sail like the wind.

'I'd like something that sails like the wind,' Alex said and she turned and gazed at her husband in astonishment. He was holding their son and looking at her with such eagerness that a bubble of laughter built within her.

'Hey, is this my present or your present?'

'Both,' he admitted. 'I figured you could build it and teach Michales and me to sail. That could be your anniversary present to us.'

'I already have an anniversary gift for you.'

'You have?' He set Michales down on his feet. 'You have a gift for me?'

'Mmm.'

'Then why are we down here when we could be back at the house opening presents?'

'This one's a work in progress,' she said. 'Like your boat.'

'A work in progress…'

'One might interrupt the other,' she said. 'I can't build two things at once. At least I don't think I can.'

'You're already building me a boat?'

'Guess again.' And she smiled at him with all the love in her heart. 'I've been building it for a couple of months now. Give me seven months more…'

He got it this time. He stared incredulously at her—and then he surged forward and lifted her high. He whirled her around and around, while Michales looked at his parents as if they'd lost their minds.

He toddled forward and Alex had to stop swinging or he'd have bowled his small son over. He set his wife down, gathered his son into his arms and then held them both. He simply held them, a man holding his family. A man granted everything he wanted in life—and more.

The terrors of the past were done. The fears. The injustices and their bitter legacy. Dispersed by love.

He loved this woman in his arms so much…

'The dolphins are watching,' Lily murmured, glancing out through the boatshed doors to where a pod of dolphins had glided into the cove, seemingly to check out what was happening.

'Let 'em look,' Alex said. 'As long as they don't have cameras. This is no time for paparazzi.'

'I wouldn't mind the odd paparazzo,' Lily murmured. 'There should be someone to document how happy I am right now.'

'There'll be enough documentation at the royal reception tomorrow,' Alex said, gathering her even more tightly into his arms. 'Meanwhile, I'll remind you every time you ask. You're asking now? I'm telling you. I love you. You're my wife. You're the mother of my children. You're my own beautiful Princess. You're my Lily and you're my love.'

MILLS & BOON®
Pure reading pleasure™

JULY 2009 HARDBACK TITLES

ROMANCE

Marchese's Forgotten Bride	Michelle Reid
The Brazilian Millionaire's Love-Child	Anne Mather
Powerful Greek, Unworldly Wife	Sarah Morgan
The Virgin Secretary's Impossible Boss	Carole Mortimer
Kyriakis's Innocent Mistress	Diana Hamilton
Rich, Ruthless and Secretly Royal	Robyn Donald
Spanish Aristocrat, Forced Bride	India Grey
Kept for Her Baby	Kate Walker
The Costanzo Baby Secret	Catherine Spencer
The Mediterranean's Wife by Contract	Kathryn Ross
Claimed: Secret Royal Son	Marion Lennox
Expecting Miracle Twins	Barbara Hannay
A Trip with the Tycoon	Nicola Marsh
Invitation to the Boss's Ball	Fiona Harper
Keeping Her Baby's Secret	Raye Morgan
Memo: The Billionaire's Proposal	Melissa McClone
Secret Sheikh, Secret Baby	Carol Marinelli
The Playboy Doctor's Surprise Proposal	Anne Fraser

HISTORICAL

The Piratical Miss Ravenhurst	Louise Allen
His Forbidden Liaison	Joanna Maitland
An Innocent Debutante in Hanover Square	Anne Herries

MEDICAL™

Pregnant Midwife: Father Needed	Fiona McArthur
His Baby Bombshell	Jessica Matthews
Found: A Mother for His Son	Dianne Drake
Hired: GP and Wife	Judy Campbell

0609 Gen Std LP

JULY 2009 LARGE PRINT TITLES

ROMANCE

Captive At The Sicilian Billionaire's Command	Penny Jordan
The Greek's Million-Dollar Baby Bargain	Julia James
Bedded for the Spaniard's Pleasure	Carole Mortimer
At the Argentinean Billionaire's Bidding	India Grey
Italian Groom, Princess Bride	Rebecca Winters
Falling for her Convenient Husband	Jessica Steele
Cinderella's Wedding Wish	Jessica Hart
The Rebel Heir's Bride	Patricia Thayer

HISTORICAL

The Rake's Defiant Mistress	Mary Brendan
The Viscount Claims His Bride	Bronwyn Scott
The Major and the Country Miss	Dorothy Elbury

MEDICAL™

The Greek Doctor's New-Year Baby	Kate Hardy
The Heart Surgeon's Secret Child	Meredith Webber
The Midwife's Little Miracle	Fiona McArthur
The Single Dad's New-Year Bride	Amy Andrews
The Wife He's Been Waiting For	Dianne Drake
Posh Doc Claims His Bride	Anne Fraser

MILLS & BOON

AUGUST 2009 HARDBACK TITLES

ROMANCE

Desert Prince, Bride of Innocence	Lynne Graham
Raffaele: Taming His Tempestuous Virgin	Sandra Marton
The Italian Billionaire's Secretary Mistress	Sharon Kendrick
Bride, Bought and Paid For	Helen Bianchin
Hired for the Boss's Bedroom	Cathy Williams
The Christmas Love-Child	Jennie Lucas
Mistress to the Merciless Millionaire	Abby Green
Italian Boss, Proud Miss Prim	Susan Stephens
Proud Revenge, Passionate Wedlock	Janette Kenny
The Buenos Aires Marriage Deal	Maggie Cox
Betrothed: To the People's Prince	Marion Lennox
The Bridesmaid's Baby	Barbara Hannay
The Greek's Long-Lost Son	Rebecca Winters
His Housekeeper Bride	Melissa James
A Princess for Christmas	Shirley Jump
The Frenchman's Plain-Jane Project	Myrna Mackenzie
Italian Doctor, Dream Proposal	Margaret McDonagh
Marriage Reunited: Baby on the Way	Sharon Archer

HISTORICAL

The Brigadier's Daughter	Catherine March
The Wicked Baron	Sarah Mallory
His Runaway Maiden	June Francis

MEDICAL™

Wanted: A Father for her Twins	Emily Forbes
Bride on the Children's Ward	Lucy Clark
The Rebel of Penhally Bay	Caroline Anderson
Marrying the Playboy Doctor	Laura Iding

0709 Gen Std LP

AUGUST 2009 LARGE PRINT TITLES

ROMANCE

The Spanish Billionaire's Pregnant Wife	Lynne Graham
The Italian's Ruthless Marriage Command	Helen Bianchin
The Brunelli Baby Bargain	Kim Lawrence
The French Tycoon's Pregnant Mistress	Abby Green
Diamond in the Rough	Diana Palmer
Secret Baby, Surprise Parents	Liz Fielding
The Rebel King	Melissa James
Nine-to-Five Bride	Jennie Adams

HISTORICAL

The Disgraceful Mr Ravenhurst	Louise Allen
The Duke's Cinderella Bride	Carole Mortimer
Impoverished Miss, Convenient Wife	Michelle Styles

MEDICAL™

Children's Doctor, Society Bride	Joanna Neil
The Heart Surgeon's Baby Surprise	Meredith Webber
A Wife for the Baby Doctor	Josie Metcalfe
The Royal Doctor's Bride	Jessica Matthews
Outback Doctor, English Bride	Leah Martyn
Surgeon Boss, Surprise Dad	Janice Lynn

12 CAP

JE